CRANES' MORNING

CRANES' MORNING

INDRANI AIKATH-GYALTSEN

BALLANTINE BOOKS

NEW YORK

Copyright © 1993 by Indrani Aikath-Gyaltsen

All rights reserved under International and Pan-American Copyright
Conventions. Published in the United States by Ballantine Books, a division of
Random House, Inc., New York, and simultaneously in Canada by Random
House of Canada Limited, Toronto. Originally published in 1993 by Penguin
Books India (P) Ltd.

The lines on page 243 are from "The Tale of the Red Rock Jewel Valley," *The
Hundred Thousand Songs of Milarepa*, vol. 5, translated and annotated by Garma
C.C. Chang, p. 5.

Library of Congress Cataloging-in-Publication Data

Aikath-Gyaltsen, Indrani, 1952–
Cranes' morning / Indrani Aikath-Gyaltsen. — 1st. American ed.
p. cm.
ISBN 0-345-38366-4
1. Country life—India—Fiction. I. Title.
PR 9499.3.A44C7 1994
823—dc20   93-22120
CIP

Manufactured in the United States of America

First American Edition: January 1994

10 9 8 7 6 5 4 3 2

Dedicated to
Sardar Khushwant Singh

CRANES' MORNING

ld Vidya sat at her window and watched the cranes with delight. It meant bad weather on this plateau when they came from the east and she had known, when she woke this morning in the waiting stillness and had seen the misted sky, that the long spell of fine weather was going to break in a rainstorm. She did not enjoy the late February winds in this drafty house whose damp and cold had already crippled her. But she enjoyed the birds and would enjoy them more when she found the right pair of spectacles. She had been reading when she first heard that strange, exciting cry and her reading glasses were no good for distance. She wasted a few precious moments finding her distance ones on the table beside her, knocking over her teacup on the breakfast tray as she did so, for her hands were knotted with arthritis. Gargi might have sharp words to say later about the dregs in the teacup staining the tray-cloth, and for a moment she flinched from the thought of them, but when she got the cranes into focus, she forgot about Gargi.

Over the valley they were weaving their patterns against the background of the terraced hills, lifting their bodies skywards. Yesterday, the terrain had had the toast-and-mustard colors of the Chotanagpur plateau in the dry season. Today it was dove grey and pearl grey with sudden splashes of an angry battleship grey. The old colors were hidden and imprisoned even as the sun was imprisoned. To Vidya the day suddenly dipped into despair. Joy sprang up at moments such as this, when the cranes wheeled and dipped, but dark pain was always behind it all. She had dreamed that the cranes would come and now that they had come, she only wanted to escape. Escape. But when there is a grey wall between one person and another, who is to say which is the prisoner and which free?

She had been obsessed by prisons and prisoners these last few days. Since she had had to lead this shut-in invalid life she had found illness involved suffering almost as much from the tyranny of painful thoughts as from physical pain. Outside this lovely valley where she lived, the world was a dreadful place and first one misery would possess her mind and then another. Crimes against children would take hold of her one day and on another she would be grieving for ill-used wives or the mad. Even if she had wanted to, she lacked the strength—that healthy bodies have—to thrust tormenting thoughts from her. And she did not want to.

The fortunate, she thought, and she counted herself fortunate, ought not to insulate themselves in their cocoons of grace. If they could do nothing else, they could steep themselves in sorrow. And pray as a last resort while grieving over the futility of prayer; she tried to make her sorrow real to herself by letting her mind bring forth one concrete fact at a time to worry about: one child in danger, some particular woman in darkness, some particular prisoner facing the world again with fear and shame. God or a blind cosmos knew who they were even if she did not! That prisoner had been with her for three days and nights now, and the greyness of this day had made him more real to her than ever. And yet she liked these grey days. They had their own beauty and their own excuses for a sick old woman. When the sun was out, the world was a young prince riding out with armor flashing and pennants flying, but on a day like this it was an old monk turned to his prayers, wrapped in a dull maroon cloak of stillness and silence.

The grey days made the perfect setting for the brilliance and freedom of the cranes. Her eyes followed their flight, the graceless obliqueness of their long, rickety legs, the slow beat of their thin wings and then a more gentle rise and fall, as though the still air had unseen waves whose rhythm rocked them. There was a great spaciousness about their jerky movements. The earth, the meandering river somewhere below, and the sky were theirs. They were content now in this valley between the hills because their wings could carry them where they would whenever they wished. Birds were more satisfactory symbols of the godly spirits than anything else, Vidya thought, though the little girls came back with stories of angels and such things from that awful school of theirs. Why wouldn't Gargi send them to the convent where the nuns taught? Everyone knew these ladies were Christians of the right kind. Anyway, there was nothing so swift and free as a bird and crippled as she was, she felt nothing but joy watching them. She had always known how to wait.

The clock on her table chimed the half-hour and her waiting was lost in sudden anxiety. Half-past-seven and no sign of Kunal bringing the car around. The children would be late for school again and would be scolded. Pia would miss the beginning of the arithmetic class and be more wretchedly bogged down in the miseries of division than ever. Rita and Gitashri would be all right because Rita's scornfulness and Gitashri's placidity usually insulated them against scoldings but their all-rightness was apt, by contrast, to make Pia the more aware of her chronic state of misfortune. It was true what the *bachans* of the scientist Khona said. People belonged to three categories—the *rakshas gan,* who bullied and browbeat their way through life; the *dev gan,* who had the capacity to rise against circumstances, and the *manushya gan,* who were, well, just human and therefore simply suffered.

Vidya listened anxiously, then relaxed as the familiar sounds of backfiring came from the garage by the hibiscus bush. Who had ever seen such a brilliant yellow in hibiscus before? Certainly not Vidya in her seventy-six years of life. The poor old car bounced out and forward, two wheels on the flower-bed and bumped slightly into a post of the porch.

Kunal drove as badly as a man can, and once he

had got the old Ford V8 as far as the cottage door
Gargi allowed him no further part in getting the girls
to school. The car was large and Gargi very petite
but she drove expertly on the isolated village roads.
Unless prevented by unavoidable crisis, she drove
the children to school herself and fetched them in
the afternoon. The nearest school that she considered worthy of her children was at Ispatpur, a small
mining town three miles down the Ruprekha river,
and that meant twelve miles driving daily and a
greater expense of time and strength and petrol than
Gargi could afford. Vidya sighed over Gargi's pride
that would not even consider the village convent,
her unpunctuality and her extravagance, and then
smiled delightedly as Gargi herself came out of the
house dressed in a cream silk daytime sari, ran down
the steps, and got into the car. At this distance she
looked the lovely girl she had been, not the
harassed, worn woman she had become at only
thirty-three; as lithe and gay as her small daughters
hurrying after her in their beige and brown uniforms. The view of all four was engaging, Vidya
thought. The girls were perfectly formed specimens
of girlhood, all thin and petite with none of the awk-
wardness or pudginess of little girls. Judging from

what the doctors said—that the height of a child of two was half of what it would be as an adult—none of the girls would be more than five feet three when they grew up. They had taken after Gargi rather than Kunal. Still, the hems of their uniforms had had to be let down.

And suddenly there were tears in her eyes. Until a couple of years ago, she had been able to do all the family mending. Four years ago, she could stand long enough to do the fine washing and ironing as well. Seven years ago, as Kunal's aunt and nominal head of the house, she had directed the household so effectively that even the impatient Gargi was impressed. Eleven years ago, when Gargi had married her distant cousin, Kunal, for some obscure reason, she, Vidya, had been sixty-five and felt fifty. Now she was seventy-six and felt ninety. Though the years of steadily increasing pain had seemed long as she endured them, in retrospect they seemed to have passed quickly. She had become imprisoned in this uselessness almost overnight, it seemed, and now she would have to bear it as well as she could. She told herself she could have put up with it better if Kunal and Gargi had done as she had told them to, and put her in an institution for such diseases which never healed, but they wouldn't hear of it. She had looked after Kunal in the big house up on the hill a mile away and his bleak childhood had been redeemed from disaster by her love. He said he could not face life without her. They all said they could not do without her. And yet Gargi would not let Pia be called by her given name "Chameli." Chameli? she would say and her delicate eyebrows would rise a fraction. "Just like a maidservant's name, isn't it?" Pia—thought Vidya, yes, it was a lovely name; but Chameli—so small and delicate and pure and white. . . .

But they all wanted her in their home; they all said they could not do without her. In the paradoxical nature of things if she believed them she would have been a much happier woman, but not the woman they could not do without.

———

The car moved down the steep, moss-grown drive and disappeared from sight in the lane that wound through the village and then along by the river to Ispatpur. Kunal stood waving to the children until he could no longer see them, and then, with his hands in his pockets and his pipe drooping from the side of his mouth, he gazed dejectedly at the view, his long figure sagging a little. He hated to see them go off to that apparently desirable school where an Armenian lady ran the show and taught, among other things, "foreign languages." Rita and Pia were not happy there though they had not told him so and Gitashri would not be when she was older. It was a small and most select school, for young children only, and rather celebrated for miles around due to the lack of any other fashionable school. But Kunal was sure it was not a good school though Gargi said it was; and with no evidence to the contrary, it was only his instinct that contradicted her. The children would have been happy at the village convent school in Mohurpukur itself but it was disliked by Gargi because such a mixture of children went there; but the Ispatpur school, coyly called "Good Start," stank in Kunal's nostrils. Yes, stank! He repeated the ugly word forcefully in his head, and then with that uncertainty and self-distrust that followed immediately upon all his actions and decisions, he retracted it. After all, what did he know about it? He had only been to the place two or three times. Gargi who went there every day, said it was all right. She should know. Mothers were more knowledgeable about little girls than fathers could hope to be. Especially when the father was such a man as himself, a negligible failure.

He took his pipe from his mouth and stared at the empty bowl. Holidays excepted, he had given up smoking for economy's sake, for Rita was to go to boarding school in the new year. He suspected she had first-class brains and he wanted to save every penny to give her her chance. But despite his resolution, in moments of perplexity, he sometimes found solace in sucking his empty pipe. That is, when he knew he was alone. He was alone now and in that fact also there was solace.

He straightened himself and became aware of the cranes. Instantly delight leaped up in him, a flame of pure joy that burned against the habitual sadness of his thoughts much as the white cranes' wings shone against the sunless landscape. Seen from this distance, the flight of the cranes was the perfection of beauty and his joy that leaped to meet it was equally perfect. Meeting, the two were one, and his joy was taken from him, the pain of its loss as sharp as the joy had been. It had been that way with him all his life, at sight or sound of beauty. The joy and then the total loss. The beauty that robbed him was, he supposed, always stronger than he, for he was a weak man. Strong men perhaps could retain the gift and give the beauty to the world again in verse or music; and from that too some other fellow would with his innate joy snatch beauty. What a divine traffic! Yet he did not regret his total loss. It was his own particular mode of giving.

Aware of a sense of companionship so delicate that it was no intrusion upon his loneliness, he looked round and up and saw Vidya's smiling face at the window. He had not seen her yet this morning. He laughed, leapt up the steps to the front door and went quickly, with a shambling but boyish stride, through the cold echoing hall, up the dark staircase and across the large drafty landing to her room. In his eagerness he hardly stopped to think why the builders of a hundred years ago were so fond of dark, unnecessary spaces. Vidya's face was like a beacon to which the grey day, his ineptness, and the thousand sorrows that sat on his shoulders year in and year out had become mere background.

"How are you, Vidi?" he asked a little anxiously. "How's the beastly pain? Did you sleep well?"

"What a man you are for asking unnecessary questions," said Vidya with annoyance. "Can't you see I'm as flourishing as a spoilt old woman can be? Sit down and eat a biscuit with honey. It's likely you prepared your notes at breakfast and forgot your food."

He laughed, sat down opposite her, and helped himself to a biscuit to please her. She smiled at him, sorry for having snapped at him.

It tried her patience if anyone inquired about her health. Monotonous daily fuss, anxiety, drove her quite distracted. Of course, she had pain and of course it kept her awake, but what of it? Did anyone expect old age to be a bed of roses? Kunal was the most trying because he loved her the most; during her bad times he went about looking more miserable than she herself ever felt. Gargi's concern tried Vidya less because it was partly for herself; the worse Vidya was the more she would have to do for her. But they both made her feel a burden when they fussed and worried. She pulled herself together. How wicked to think of burdens on this still and peaceful morning, with the birds there. They were no burden to the air that supported them, nor the air to the fields to which it brought the sunshine and the rain. There should be no thought of burdens on a morning such as this, when the grey stillness had such beauty. She then found herself wondering if the weakness in oneself that pressed most heavily on others wasn't a blessing after all; and if the occasions when one thought one was doing great good were actually moments of great harm, especially if self-congratulation was present.

She smiled at Kunal, who, so far as she knew, had never congratulated himself upon anything whatsoever, and wondered to what extent his lifelong sense of failure was his greatest asset. She could not know. No one could know, least of all Kunal. All she knew was the love it had opened up in her from the day she had arrived at the "Big House," and found the little boy of three sobbing in a dark corner of his room with his paternal aunt, Kanan, wringing her hands in loving desperation—Kanan who could cope so well with everything in the world except the death of Kunal's parents, or rather Kunal's grief at their loss in an accident. Looking at him now she marveled at how little he had changed in over forty years. He was stooped and careworn, his hair greying and receding at the temples, his face overweighed by his longish nose, mouth a little open because everything was a cause of wonder to him; but his eager impulsive movements, ending generally in disaster and combining so well with the Kushari charm and distinction, his smile and anxious clear grey eyes, were exactly the same as when she had first known him.

He too was thinking how little she had changed. Her dark eyes had never lost their brightness nor her small, determined face its clear contours. She had always been a sallow, plain little woman, quite a contrast, he was told, to Kunal's own mother, her sister. Vidya's charm lay in her birdlike quickness, her vitality and humor. The wrinkling of the skin and the whitening of her hair had changed her very little. "The cranes are here, Vidi," he said. "That means a storm before night."

"I knew there was a change coming when I woke this morning," said Vidya. "And not only in the weather."

"Change for us all?" asked Kunal. "How do you know these things, Vidya?"

"I couldn't rightly say," said Vidya, "but don't you feel it yourself? The pause. The shuttle goes backwards and forwards, much the same year after year, and then the pause, like a hand wavering over a workbasket looking for a new color to thread into the fabric of our days."

"Dull old sticks like myself don't feel these things," said Kunal. "Though I've often thought migratory birds have news to tell of a pattern somewhere, when they weave in and out like that."

They smiled at each other, remembering Kunal's

childhood days at the Big House when they had
watched the birds together. On those occasions they
had looked down on them from a height, and seen
the Ruprekha river winding like a ribbon through
the valley, and the village so far below it looked like
a toy village. Sometimes a strong, solitary bird
would break away from the others and fold its wings
on top of the Big House and that had always thrilled
Kunal.

"What are you going to do today?" asked Vidya
with a touch of sharpness. She was always keeping
him up to it, and so was Gargi, for his conviction
that whatever he did he'd be sure to make a mess of
it would often make him shrink from action. It
wasn't that he was lazy. Physical inertia was a thing
he fought successfully and at lonely tasks he would
work untiringly. It was personal contacts—whether
with his students or with people at the university
whom he had to go to for grants for his little private
college—that terrified him, and a college principal's life seemed full of them. His conviction that he
was a very bad teacher and should never have been
one he kept to himself, for it was too late now and
useless remorse should not be inflicted on others;
but like the worst kind of wound, it bled inwardly.

"Take my tray down, to save Gargi's time,"

Vidya said to him. "She has an extra busy day today. She has to organize the staff wives' tea, a thing she hates."

"So do I. Have an extra busy day. They say old Kishun, Aunt Kanan's cowman, is poorly."

"The old curmudgeon," said Vidya.

"That doesn't prevent him being poorly," he replied.

"He hates busybodies pushing in on him," said Vidya and continued, "he's cantankerous and so there won't be anyone to walk the heights up to his lodge and maybe get the door shut in their faces for their pains. But he always likes a Kushari. And he likes a drop of brandy."

"Where will I get the brandy?" Kunal asked.

"In the wardrobe, behind my shawls," said Vidya. "You can take a look if you don't believe me. If you don't get out of that chair you won't get anything done today."

Kunal walked to the wardrobe, looked behind her shawls, and whistled incredulously.

"I've had it for two years now. Your Aunt Kanan gave it to me along with a silver flask. For the pain she said. The brandy was from your grandfather's stock. But don't take the silver flask. Take the other small tea flask. You can fill that for Kishun."

"This is the first time you've suggested I should encourage the villagers in secret drinking," said Kunal. But he did as she told him, subduing the revulsion that the smell of any form of alcohol invariably gave him. He always did as Vidya told him. She had a shrewd knowledge of human nature and an almost uncanny instinct for knowing just the thing to say, the thing to do, that would open a door and not close it.

"Kishun's no drunkard," said Vidya. "Too stingy. But he likes comfort if another pays for it." And, then she said, digressing: "I've always noticed from the old days in the Big House that when a man takes against religion, it's small comforts that he fancies that can get him back to religion."

"Worldly wisdom, Vidya," said Kunal, picking up the flask by its long plastic handle.

"I've no other," said Vidya briefly, but she gave him a delightful smile as he picked up her tray. It was a smile that he had known well since his boyhood. Vidya had never praised him in words, but with that particular smile she both recognized merit and rewarded it. He had the other sort of wisdom, her smile told him now. He did not believe her but her smile was the balm it had always been.

"Anything I can do before I go?"

"You can turn the television on," said Vidya, "and when Rampujari comes," she said, referring to the daily help, "tell her to soak the tray-cloth. I've spilt tea on it." Their eyes met involuntarily, for both of them dreaded an annoyed Gargi, but loyalty did not allow the glance to linger long enough to create mutual sympathy.

Kunal carried the tray down the dark stairs to the kitchen. It was a dreary, stone-floored place where the aroma of mice fought daily with the slightly unsanitary smell of the drains. However much Gargi opened the windows or lit an *angiti* instead of using gas, she could never quite get rid of the smells, for the damp of the kitchen imprisoned them. The walls were stained with damp for the kitchen was built against an embankment and there was said to be an old, disused spring under the kitchen floor. No one knew for sure, not even his Aunt Kanan, but Gargi had stormed once, "Move the kitchen just eight yards to the east. We can grow herbs where it stands now. Surely we can run to that much money. Surely Aunt Kanan could sell the outhouses at the Big House. Surely . . ." Soon after, the kitchen had been improved as much as possible. There was a new Mona Lisa stove, bright electric lights, and Gargi had strung the walls with copper-bottomed pots and pans. There were pots of geraniums here and there and a Bengal Pottery copy of the famous willow pattern plate set in blue and white. Yet, it remained a dreary cave, a symbol somehow of the whole cottage, a house that was too large to be called a cottage, yet too small for them all, with no working space, too dark, too damp, ever to make a comfortable home. To make matters worse, he and Gargi were not as happy as they had promised to be in each other though they loved their children. It couldn't be altogether the fault of the house, and he refused to admit any fault in Gargi. It must be his fault. He had failed in marriage, as in everything else. A feeling of hopelessness woke in him and he put the tray down on a nearby ledge at an angle; the teapot rolled off it and was smashed on the stone floor.

The crash restored him, and for very shame he battened down the depression that had caused it. If he could not measure up to the big demands life made upon him, if he were a poor professor, an unsatisfactory husband and father, he might at least endeavor to be competent as "a hewer of wood and drawer of water." And he could be so on the rare occasions when he managed to get his worried mind really focused upon what he was doing, for he enjoyed trivial tasks. Once intent upon them, the rhythm of the work swung his mind free of himself; but that first concentration, like a tunnel that carries a man through darkness to fresh air and sunlight, was not easy for him.

Today he managed it. He took off his jacket, rolled up his sleeves, lifted up to Providence the magnitude of his failure and the triviality of his task, and applied himself to the latter. The cold water at first felt chill on his hands, later the circulation got going and the pile of cleansed china grew satisfactorily on the draining-board. There was pleasure in getting things clean and pleasure in the thought of pleasing both Gargi and the overworked Rampujari. Small beauties slid one by one into his consciousness quietly and unobtrusively like growing light. The sinuous curves of the cat who was simply called Cat, the comfortable soft sound of ash settling in the *angiti,* a woodpecker worrying at the bark of a tree somewhere, the pungent smell of Gargi's geraniums, the gold of the crocuses that were growing around the trunk of the gulmohur tree outside the kitchen window. . . . What in the name of wonder had happened to it? He knew its fantastic beauty of old, and he thought he knew it by heart, but he had never seen it quite like this; it was shamelessly, embarrassingly beautiful. He went on with the washing-up deftly and surely, for the rhythm of the work had taken charge, quite unconsciously; and joy leaped up in him again, a joy even greater than when he had seen the cranes.

The gulmohur tree was a personality older than the house, short by tree standards and twisted and encrusted with lichen, its widely spread roots clutching the earth with the splayed feet of a giant, its trunk knobby with knotholes, its branches flung crazily skyward like a madman praying. It was a travesty of a tree, like a bonsai grown out of control, its very shapelessness like the bones of the earth. But it was always beautiful. In March the new green leaves were sharp and delicate, a mist of pale green and then with a rush came the vociferous red-gold color, blotting out the shape of the branches, the dim outline of the tree's skeleton taking its leave in a colored flood of flowers. But though the leaves had not emerged yet, Kunal had never seen it look so amazingly lovely as it did today. The whole tree was a black tracery against the grey of the day, sparkling and bleak yet so gentle that it did not blind his eyes. Its clean clear silveriness washed into the dark, smelly, old kitchen like a wave of sea-water washing into a cave, in and out again, cleansing it. And the pale grey light, composed of the myriad, minute globes of water with which the mist had spangled every twig, never left the tree. The sun had come out for a moment and been reborn, a microcosm of itself, in the heart of each globe.

"My God," ejaculated Kunal. It was not a profane exclamation but an acknowledgment of a miracle and a revelation.

"Dirty day," said Rampujari, divesting herself of her shawl, old rubber slippers, and straightening her nose-ring. Kunal turned round and met her pitying glance. His extraordinarily sweet smile flashed out in welcome. He had, he knew, been gazing at the gulmohur tree with his mouth more than usually open, like a small boy contemplating fireworks, but he was unabashed. He knew that his villagers, of whom he was the last of the so-called zamindars, considered him to be more than a little eccentric. All that book learning; certainly they regarded him as being not quite so mentally all there as they were themselves, but he was so chronically aware himself of his total inadequacy that the awareness of others of this fact did not worry him. Indeed, he was glad of it, for it prevented them placing him upon some pedestal removed from the humdrum happenings of their daily lives.

Turning his back on the gulmohur tree he

propped himself against the sink for the preliminary gossip before the morning's work, without which Rampujari did not function. It was to her as oil to a machine and she could not get started without it. Gargi, with a multitude of tasks of her own awaiting attention, was always trying to escape, but Kunal agreed tacitly with Rampujari that it was ridiculous to make such a fetish of housework as Gargi did. What did a little dust matter? The communing of one soul with another was really more important, even if it were only on the subject of mice or chronic coughs and colds.

He thought to himself now that it did not much matter in itself, what one did. It was chiefly as the vehicle of love or as a symbol of communication that action was important or did he only think that because in action he was himself generally such a bungler? Perhaps if he faced the truth he would find that one of the reasons he spent so much time in contemplation was because the results of contemplation were unknown and one could not go wrong with what never happened except in the mind. It was just bread cast upon the waters, without hope or desire for knowledge or reward. It is difficult, he thought, for a human being to face the fact that he is really quite superfluous.

". . . And so it's scarcely Bachua's fault really," said Rampujari. "Not with the nut working loose. He did feel the wheel wobble like, but as I said to his father, you can't expect an old head on young shoulders. Of course it's a loss, all these eggs and the money. . . ."

"Rampujari, I do beg your pardon but I am afraid I was wool-gathering," said Kunal apologetically. "Which was the nut that worked loose?"

Gargi, when she lost the thread, just made what she hoped were appropriate noises, but Kunal, though he did most things badly, always did them to the best of his ability. Deeply ashamed, he braced himself more firmly against the sink and tried to rivet his attention upon Rampujari's narrative. One of these days someone would be telling him something really important and disaster would come upon them all because he had missed the first half. In any case, how could he know that this narrative of Rampujari's was not important? It might, for all he knew, have a great bearing upon all their lives. Though it is true that for the power of whatever divine law that guides us all things are superfluous, it is also true that for the mercy of Providence nothing is. Every sparrow, every hair, every soul, every nut. Only he wished he could believe it, but after having

Gargi would be so busy. On the way to the tube-roses he was distressed by the sight of a dead sparrow lying on the lawn. Shame upon Cat. Well fed though he was, he did occasionally forget himself and kill from wanton cruelty. A stab of pain went through Kunal as he bent and picked up the small body, still warm. "Not a sparrow falls to the ground"—rubbish. Look at this sparrow, look at him, look at his color. The little bird wore a sober livery and in the company of a kingfisher or a parakeet, one would not have looked at him twice, yet lying there in his palm he seemed to Kunal incomparably beautiful. The back and wing feathers were of different shades of brown, tender, warm tobacco colors, the throat and soft breast like the smoke that escapes from an industrial chimney and becomes muted just before it reaches the far sky. A short while ago, the eyes had been as bright as the drops of water on the gulmohur tree, but now they were filmed over. He would not again utter his thin, irritating song. Kunal had what Gargi considered a ridiculous, inordinate love of the creatures. When he came to himself he was out in the lane, the small corpse still in his hand.

His idea, he believed, had been to carry it right

learned comparative religion for six years an
it for twenty more, he had grown skeptical. A
sad panorama of human woes that passed daily
his eyes . . .

". . . And then, of course, he had to swer
rickshaw to the left or else he'd have run the
chap down. And that must have jolted the nut
You know Bachua's three-wheel rickshaw with
tray behind? And so all the eggs broke. Dread
thing, drink. Not Bachua, the stranger. Where
he get it, so early in the morning? Good clothes,
was wearing too. And I must say he tried to help Ba
chua but suddenly came over queer. And what could
he do? After all, broken eggs are broken eggs. Just
by the Crooked Bridge it was and Bachua late already. Well Babu Sahib, I'll see to your aunt. Make
her comfortable like and then start the lunch."

Kunal put away the clean crockery and carried
the broken teapot out to the dust bin, where he hid
it from Gargi's sight beneath a couple of empty tins,
and then, ashamed of such deception, fished it out
again and placed it where she would be sure to see
it. "Teapots of a size for just one person are impossible to buy," he had heard her say. Oh, well!

He went into the garden to cut flowers for the
staff room; the wives' tea would be held there and

out of the garden so that Gitashri should not find it and grieve, for Gitashri felt like her father about the creatures. He glanced round for somewhere to put it, but then his eye was caught by the lovely loops of the Ruprekha river, meandering away down the valley. Through a break in the trees he could see it clearly and the Mohurpukur village proper. Now what had Rampujari been saying about Crooked Bridge? Something about a drunken stranger whose staggering had caused young Bachua to have an accident with the egg rickshaw. Probably Bachua's fault for he never looked where he was going. Rampujari might consider him a good boy but Kunal did not. He had seen him tying a can to a dog's tail once. Kunal for once had exercised his prerogative as the village landlord and spanked Bachua. Just like Bachua, the rascal, to leave the drunk who had tried to help him with his wheel to stagger around a new place without assistance.

Kunal stood in the middle of the lane and fought one of the dreaded battles that he had to combat almost daily. The sweat broke out on his forehead and his fingers clenched upon the dead bird. He was too ashamed of these paltry battles to speak of them. Since his boyhood he had been plagued by ridiculous obsessions, childish fears and torments of all sorts. He had once heard his aunt Kanan who was his guardian tell Vidya that he suffered from "inner bissions"; later he learned the word was "inhibitions." During his student days in Calcutta he had been able to keep them firmly battened down; it was only since his college was in such dire straits that they had thrust themselves out again in new forms but with all their old strength. This particular obsession, however, the dread of a drunken man, was not much altered since his childhood, when he had to be kept out of his father's way. Yet it had been altered; its present edge of intensity had been given to it by some appalling months during his Ph.D. research course when he had fought his father's demon in himself. How it had happened that he had come out victorious, he had no idea. He had no idea, either, how he came out upon the other side of these ridiculous, contemptible struggles. It was rather like a painful sojourn at the dentist's. You endured, apparently for an eternity, and then it was over but not due to any action of your own.

It was over and he was walking down the lane towards the road beside the river. He was vaguely aware of a cat flashing by towards the old buildings that formed the college campus. He turned to the left and went resolutely loping on beside the river, towards Crooked Bridge and the highway that met the village road a mile ahead to the left. He was still holding the dead bird.

CHAPTER TWO

*V*ikram leaned his arms on the parapet of the
bridge, watching the eddying waters. The attack of
dizziness had passed. He was all right as long as he
kept still, merely feeling a bit light-headed. The sensation was pleasant rather than otherwise, for it was
a dreamy light-headedness that softened the edges of
things. Past and future no longer pressed sharply
upon him and the moment was shot through with incredible beauty. It flowed into him through sight and
sound and even the touch of the rough stone parapet
filled him with such an airy lightness that he seemed
to float even while the rough stone supported him.
He felt like a small child being swung by a beloved
adult, in delicious danger and delicious safety at the
same time.

Below him the river was greenish and clear,
faintly flecked with the light of a clouded day. He

was glad there was no sun to sparkle too brightly on
the water. He liked it like this. The water wound
away through the lovely valley very quietly, making
no sound except where its eddies chuckled about the
piers of the bridge. Upon either side of the valley the
fields lifted to the sal woods. Their color seemed
brave to him but he had heard that even the heat of
an Indian summer did not daunt them. For him the
green was a laughing green and the color of the
plowed fields a brown song. But the laughter and the
song were distant; what was near was the voice of
the water about the piers of the bridge and the snap
of the cranes' wings all about him. They were silent
now, weren't cranes always supposed to be silent?
Those that were over the river were dipping and
wheeling and soaring silently, those in the fields
were facing into the wind and gliding along as
though the ridges of the plowed land were the waves
of an inland sea. Against the deep brown of the
turned earth their wings gleamed like snow—snow
that was a little dirty, as when a salt plow has been
over it; and when he looked up he could see clearly
the grey feathers among the white, that same exquis-
ite mother-of-pearl grey of the sky. And their flight!
The freedom that was in those sweeping curves. The
freedom of the water flowing unchecked to some

bigger river, like a relay race. The freedom of the lifting fields and the hills that swelled against the sky. The ecstasy of this freedom was such music in his blood that his whole body pulsed with intense joy. It was the beat of this joy in freedom that kept him swinging in light even while the stone of the parapet gripped his right hand that was laid upon it.

The throbbing increased and became an almost monotonous drumming. It thrummed in his head, too, and behind his eyes, and pounded in his chest. He could no longer hear the water, only the ugly hammering in his ears and the monotonous steps coming down the passage to take him away. The light in which he had swung was coagulating to darkness. He clutched at a hand that should have been there but was not. He turned, groping for it, and the ground slid away like surf beneath his feet. He would have fallen had he not found another hand, or rather it found him, gripping his arm.

"Hold on," said a startled voice, with no confidence in it, "steady, now. This way and you can sit down." He was soon sitting down on a milestone by the bridge, very uncomfortably.

"Take a pull at this disgusting liquid," said the voice again. "It won't do you any harm for I doubt if you're drunk."

Vikram took a gulp of what was offered to him and then pushed away the plastic glass gently.

"Certainly not," he said. Then he smiled, "At least I wasn't but I am now. That's very good brandy." For even the small dose he had had, on a completely empty stomach, had sent the world reeling round him again. But he was aware that he was under scrutiny and was not surprised when the voice said, "When was your last meal?"

"This morning," said Vikram.

"Liar," said the voice equably. "Stay where you are. I won't be a moment."

———

Vikram stayed where he was. Coming down the road he had noticed a *dhaba,* which had come alive with their fires and large cooking utensils. It catered to the highway, he gathered, and also that that was where the voice had gone. He had gazed longingly at it but a bed at the retiring room at the station, a toothbrush, toothpaste, razor, and soap had taken the last of his cash. There were only a few coins left in his pocket. What a crazy fool he had been! The fumes of the brandy slowly cleared from his mind, and sitting now withdrawn within himself, behind his shuttered lids, the beauty that had so exalted him was shut out and the fool that he had been yesterday, and always, was very much with him. He had completely lost control of himself yesterday. Damn, cowardly fool. Just because he had seen a gleam of recognition in the eyes of a man he had known he must bolt as senselessly as a terrified rabbit driven out of the last of the standing corn!

It was then that he had lost his nerve. He had gone straight to the station, without even going back to his apartment, and caught a southeastern express. He could not take up work again in Calcutta and meet the contempt and accusation of men and women he had known. A brave man would have faced it or a man who was morally guiltless. Not merely legally guiltless. So he'd run away. Taken a ticket for that place in the southwest whose name for some reason attracted him. Mohurpukur. It was not even in his state. Yet it had sounded like a bit of Bengal. Mohurpukur. And he had read of it somewhere. Something to do with a family of educationists, do-gooders. He had never forgotten the name. While in the law courts, giving evidence, the name would resound, far away, like a dream bell or harps in heaven. And now he was here. Without money all virtue had gone out of Mohurpukur. It was a tiresome, if temporary mess. When he had arrived there in the dawn, it had seemed a paradise, but later as he got hungrier and realized his predicament, it was just a little muffosil town like millions in India. He had walked from the station along what seemed to be the main road until his attack of dizziness had almost upset the egg three-wheeler. Then upon the bridge had come that strange, almost anguished experience of incomparable beauty. That had been paradise for a moment or two. But what now? Where did one go from here? Any grain of common sense that he might have had in the past was now entirely lost.

"A paratha, some cold chicken curry, and tea. My own breakfast was a bit sketchy. We'll share it, shall we? You don't see a dead bird anywhere about, do you?"

Vikram drank some tea from the thick glass which his host offered him, devoured the cold chicken enclosed in a thick paratha like a famished, pariah dog, and then inquired, "What did you say? I don't think I quite understood."

"No matter," said the vague and gentle voice. "I was carrying a dead sparrow, but I seem to have mislaid it." A bit cracked, thought Vikram, as he reached for another paratha roll. Yet sufficiently intelligent to have produced a thoroughly good meal.

And probably not as mentally gone as he was himself.

"Did you want it?" he asked politely. "Might I have some more tea?"

"Take the other glass. Oh, there it is on the bridge. I must have laid it there. The bird I mean, not the tea. Excuse me a moment." He picked up something tenderly, brought it back and showed it to Vikram.

"A sparrow," said Kunal. "These dull-colored birds are the most beautiful, don't you think? I'd rather have that little chap than a kingfisher any day."

Kunal picked up a leaf from the ground, a bright-green perfectly shaped sal, laid the bird gently upon it, walked down the bank to the river and launched the small boat upon the waters. Borne by the current it floated slowly away.

"The Lady of Shallot," said Vikram, a little breathless with suppressed laughter.

"I think it was a man," said Kunal with extreme gravity. "Though there's so little difference in the plumage that it's difficult to tell."

"I know," said Vikram weakly. "It was the boat that made me think of that lovelorn lady, 'The broad beam bore her far away, the Lady of Shallot.'" He suppressed the last of his laughter. It was unkind to laugh at these amiable lunatics, and especially this one, for when he had stooped from his great spindly height he had looked exactly like Vikram's idea of Don Quixote, "the luminary and mirror of all knight-errantry"—a gentle and melancholy knight for whom Vikram had the greatest affection. Indeed, Quixote was almost his favorite character in literature. . . . And he had been created by a man in prison . . . where Vikram himself had gone. The thought of the great Cervantes, "the maimed perfection," and of his sufferings so triumphantly endured, was one of the things that had helped to keep the skeptical Vikram sane many times. He was young enough to believe that men may go mad and that men die more easily than in fact they do. He put the point where endurance is no longer possible at a reasonable distance along the way, not at the distant point where Kunal could have told him that it does in fact exist.

"It would be such a pity if a child saw it," explained Kunal. "They grieve over these things."

"There you're wrong," said Vikram bitterly. "Children are heartless little beasts. Compassion is a late development. If it develops at all."

Kunal turned round, his lean face alight with

amusement. "You're still young. So is my wife. Younger than you in fact. She talks like you."

When Kunal was amused, his smile was like wintry sunshine. His cadaverous boniness was suddenly transformed with brilliant promise like a dry twig blossoming into an unexpected flower upon the instant.

Vikram was taken aback by the promise. He said with quick humility, "I've eaten all the food. And you've paid for it. That, I imagine, is typical."

"Of what?" asked Kunal.

"Of the kind of man you are. Of the kind of man I am."

"It's early days to pass judgment on each other," said Kunal. "Though in any case I think that's an unprofitable employment. Human character is so full of surprises. Even those one knows best continually surprise one." He paused. "And in the things one does sometimes, the thoughts one has, one surprises oneself most of all. Invariably unpleasantly."

"There you're right," said Vikram, shortly, grimly, and desperately.

Kunal sat down beside him, absentmindedly pulled out his empty pipe, and sucked at it. He was remembering what Vidya had said this morning. "A new color being threaded in for a new pattern." He gazed straight in front of him, but did not see the birds riding the muddy dark sea of the plowed fields, the sight that was once more absorbing Vikram. He saw instead, as clearly as though he looked upon a painted portrait, the face of the man beside him. He had always had this queer visual gift. He could take in, with a few quick glances, every detail of a face, and then see it again as though memory were a lantern that projected the picture upon the vastness of his compassion. He would not have so explained it to himself. His love for humanity, existing side by side with his self-distrustful shrinking from them when they were not actually confronting him; and his fellow feeling for them that had been bled white and stretched taut with use, were remarkable, but had not been remarked upon by himself.

Though he could not trust his own judgement, he nevertheless knew men, and the face he was looking at both interested and touched him. It was the face of a fairly young man, though not so young as his bitterness had first led him to expect. About forty, nearly his own age he realized with a start. It was a brittle-looking, charming face, thin and fair, with a certain childishness about it that was contradicted by the weariness of the eyes and the weather-beaten appearance of the skin. It was a weak face, obstinately and rather angrily set in repose but with a delightful puckish humor breaking through when he laughed or spoke. His hair was long and rough like the fur of an infuriated animal. In his lithe wiriness, wariness, and hungriness, he reminded Kunal of a stray dog that had never known kindness and chose to bark at would-be rescuers. Not that there was any sign of barking at the moment, but any attempt at rescuing would undoubtedly produce it. The man wore good, well-made clothes but seemed the untidy type. Wrinkled socks and a scarf askew were obviously a part of his temperament. But a good shave and clean hands were a part of his temperament too, and those with well-cut clothes and imported scarves in a poor country are seldom the sort of types who starve.

"What is the matter? And what do I do?" wondered Kunal in an appalling state of worry. It was perpetually his duty given his own nature as well as the fact that he was first-gentleman of Mohurpukur to do the right thing by everybody. That he succeeded was seldom apparent to him. And he liked this man, not only because of his characteristic love of mankind but with an intense personal sympathy as well. Kunal thought him not yet an adult. Most probably the child in him had not been able to meet the challenge with which life confronts a man. He might spit defiance with an angry attempt at courage, he might swagger along with an apparent crust of toughness, but any sudden test would shatter the crust. In the depths of his failure he would know an exceedingly bitter shame. Kunal almost sweated in sympathy. It might have been himself leaning there. . . . One had to do something, no matter how futile. One had to stick like a burr and as irritatingly. It was the other chap who had to do the pulling off, when he could no longer stand the irritation.

"Now what do we do?" he asked, and his grey eyes, as he turned them on Vikram, were full of bewilderment. Vikram laughed and a most invigorating sense of strength came to him. This chap seemed even more incompetent than he was himself. Any appeal for help always touched and sated him as nothing else did. It was so rare.

"I go on my way and you go on yours," he suggested. "That is you go on to Mohurpukur and I go wherever this road's leading to."

"I wasn't going back to Mohurpukur," said Kunal, "I was coming to find you and if you're going to where this road leads to, it's Ispatpur. On the edges of Mohurpukur, I have an errand and we'll go together." He sighed with relief as he unfolded himself and stood up. So far, so good. The next ten minutes of their existence were mapped out for them.

"Nothing to worry about for ten minutes," he said, "fifteen if we go slowly."

"Should we make it twenty and return the glasses and this utensil to the *dhaba*?" suggested Vikram.

Kunal looked at him with admiration. "I should have forgotten them," he said.

"You stay here," said Vikram. "I'll take them."

Kunal did as he was told. The initiative had passed now to the other man and he rejoiced in nothing so much as in obedience. But when Vikram came back he was once more sucking at his empty pipe because he had just remembered that he had forgotten to tell Rampujari to wash the tray-cloth.

"Are you temporarily out of tobacco or do you prefer it that way?" asked Vikram as they strolled companionably down the road.

"Except on holidays I don't smoke now," said Kunal, "it's not necessary. But my pipe has become a habit with me. I pull at it without thinking about what I am doing." He put it away. "And it's not necessary."

"In this damnable world smoking is most necessary," said Vikram, and offered a leather cigarette case with one cigarette in it. Kunal stopped dead in horror, about to protest, for the cigarette cried aloud to him that it had been kept for a particularly bad moment. Then he took it, and felt at once in his own being the balm he had given to the spirit of the other. In terms of sacrifice the meal was now more than paid for.

"What did you mean, that you were coming to look for me?" asked Vikram as they strolled on again. "How did you know I was draped over the bridge?"

"The egg-cart. It could not deliver today."

"I am sorry," said Vikram. "And I was reported drunk? Have you any particular affection for drunkards?"

"Not at all. But I'm sort of the landlord of this little place, you know."

"I didn't know," said Vikram. "Of Ispatpur too?"

"No, not Ispatpur, I'd be rich if I were."

"But what a sense of duty! You must be much occupied."

Kunal was delighted to see that the man was enjoying himself, pulling his leg. His impish humor was now entirely in the ascendant and he seemed to have shed ten years as he laughed. But why was he drifting along the roads of the world in this hungry, well-dressed, and peculiar fashion?

"What is your attitude towards the inquisitive?" asked Kunal anxiously.

"I knock them down," said Vikram.

"You have a fine imagination," stated Kunal gently.

"Is that so obvious?" asked Vikram.

"A deduction from your policy to exaggeration," said Kunal. "You will like Mohurpukur and Ispatpur too, for they have their exaggerations also. My great-granduncle thought Mohurpukur was like a bit of Bengal; probably because of the Ruprekha river suddenly stopping its dance to form pools. But Ispatpur—no, he would not buy land there. Only stones under the surface and which crop would grow on stone? So he spent a fortune beautifying Mohurpukur and let the iron mine go. The village still remembers him and calls him the 'mad zamindar.' His house, the Big House, is at the top of that incline there."

"Do you live there?" asked Vikram.

"No. My paternal aunt, the mad zamindar's granddaughter lives there. My grandfather spent his fortune on a graduate college, a private college. I teach there. I am also by way of being its principal.

Our staff live around; they are mostly locals. A total of seven.''

''Is your aunt as mad as your great-granduncle?''

Kunal considered the question seriously, striving for a truthful answer. ''I think most people would consider her to be unusual,'' he said. ''I don't. I did not consider my great-granduncle mad; only a little peculiar at times. I think the fact of the matter is that we are rather an odd family, but we seem quite normal to each other.''

Vikram was chuckling now, his eyes twinkling. Talking to this Mad Hatter of a zamindar-professor was the first entertaining thing that had happened to him in years. First that experience of beauty upon the bridge, then a good meal, and now this comic relief. Where exactly was this lost valley, ringed about with these hills? It was not in any world that he knew. In what country did a river of mother-of-pearl tinged with aquamarine slip between banks of a papery flower with berries of black, the name of which he did not know, while up above them an old woman with great diamonds in her ears lived with her decadence in the splendid dust of a ruined house and walked (probably) the tangled path of a mad garden full of roses, now turned briar? In no country of concrete experience, only in some country his soul knew and longed for. If Kunal had the gift of re-creating before his mind's eye a face he had seen in a few quick glances, Vikram, out of chance phrases and flashes of intuition, had always in the old days been able to build for himself his country of escape. But his imagination had always been dependent upon exterior beauty. Cervantes? He must have known the same country and had doubtless retained the power to create it even surrounded by prison walls, so great were his own interior riches. But Vikram's imagination had always been dependent upon exterior beauty, and cut off from that he had been cut off from his dream country too.

"These berries of flame, rose and gold, do they turn black at last?"

"Yes. Are you fond of gardens? Don't worry. It is a gambit of mine, asking people if they are fond of gardens. Only a rhetorical question."

"So it can be answered," replied Vikram. "I know how to prune roses to an outward-facing bud and that most plants turn towards the sun. Could you find me a job? Why, what's the matter?"

"The cut flowers," said Kunal miserably. "I had to take them to the staff drawing-room. My wife will be expecting them."

They were nearly at the gates of a small building,

obviously a college and Kunal strode along so fast that it wasn't worth Vikram's effort to keep up with this miserable mad professor.

"Good-bye and thank you," said Vikram. He held out his hand but the professor did not take it. The distress upon his face struck Vikram first as comic and then as profoundly moving. The man looked as Pharaoh might have looked watching the death of his first-born, his grief carved upon the high nobility of his aquiline face and biting inward, so that the lines of the face sharpened, the hollows deepened. And all because he could not take a vagabond stranger to his home for fear of his wife probably. Vikram formed a quick mental picture of his helper's wife; sharp, shrewish, one who insisted that her husband's quixotic charity function out of doors only. Of the mental suffering of a truly compassionate mind, Vikram was not aware. All the same he was moved to pity for a man who had not the courage to say "come home with me" and take the consequences with his wife.

"My name is Vikram Sen," he said, pronouncing the words with almost a touch of insolence. "Vikram Sen. You don't know it, of course," he added with bravado, and then, meeting Kunal's eyes where dwelt nothing but a puzzled expression, he nearly choked on a sudden burst of laughter at himself; for both insolence and bravado had been quite unnecessary. Vikram Sen had never been heard of in this lost valley. Or else he had never been so important in any valley at all. But the professor was hurrying away, full of distress. "I will not leave Mohurpukur without seeing you again," Vikram promised, whether himself or his host, he could not say.

Kunal turned in at the gate of his own home. He felt that the man would keep his promise and was reassured in a corner of his mind. Then he broke into a loping run towards the house, unearthed the pair of scissors especially kept for cutting flowers, and began cutting flowers with the headlong haste of remorse.

Powerless to stop him, Vidya watched from the window, as she had watched Gargi cutting with the haste of anger. To Gargi she had longed to cry, "Give him time to remember," and to Kunal she wanted to say, "Give her time to forget."

They never gave each other time. The nervous irritation of the one and the nervous anxiety of the other, meeting head-on were the source of all their clashes. "Nerves," thought Vidya, "we never had them when I was young. We couldn't afford them.

But could Kunal or Gargi either? Dear God, why couldn't they laugh at each other.''

———

Annoyance never impaired Gargi's artistic skill. With her whole being flaming with resentment at Kunal's forgetfulness, the boredom of the village, the shabbiness of the house, the never-ending work in the house and in the college, her own insufficient strength, she could nevertheless arrange larkspurs and gladioli along with the bulrushes and stiff palm as no other woman could arrange them: beautifully, delicately; something of her own beauty seemed to fuse into theirs, her conscious life mingling with their unconscious being, so that it seemed that they took of her striving towards perfection and made it their own, and gave her in exchange something of their own serene obedience to the law of their being. . . . Gradually as she worked, her resentment died away, almost as if it seeped out of her fingers, and acquiescence took its place. It was quiet in the staff drawing-room and she heard a bird laughing. Every bird that laughed she thought of as a kookaburra. Certainly not a mockingbird—and she was sure the mockingbird did not mock.

She had always had this gift of correspondence with natural beauty, especially with plants and flowers. It was not the same thing as Kunal's gift of sympathy with creatures and humanity that caused him so much pain, for in her correspondence there was only pleasure. Her pain came from inside herself, from her resentment of the contrariness and frustrations of life, while his grew out of watching an external panorama of grief, growing inevitably from his compassion. It was a simplification of the difference between them to say that to the selfish comfort comes from the external things, while to the selfless consolation comes interiorly, but that was the way Gargi put it to herself. She revered her husband even when he drove her to distraction.

She finished arranging her flowers, slipped into the chair in which she was used to sitting during the staff teas. It was always to her own seat that she gravitated when she found herself alone in this room. She had no love for that particular chair; it had been especially designed to produce a maddening ache in her back but it was hers, the cranny in the rock that was her appointed place, and unconsciously she clung to it. She was as restless as any of Kunal's birds, beating her wings against the bars of her mistaken marriage but perversely she clung to such mental rocks as this particular chair. It must remain unchangeable if wild creatures like herself were always to find it there, as she must stay where she was for her children's sake, her little girls whom she had not much wanted. She did not like girls—or women either, for that matter. She was a man's woman and had longed with desperation for a son.

Why must a principal's wife always be expected to be present at every minor college event? But here she was, lodged in her own particular cranny within the permanence of the small world she belonged to. She remembered a verse from her convent school days, one of those hymns the nuns taught—"Rock of ages cleft for me"—was there only so much to life and to living? There was that laughing-bird again. Forget about the tea, forget everything. Now that the anger had passed, she was feeling peaceful, she who was always so depressed and restless. Seeds blow into crannies, you know, shapeless blown atoms that bloom into the wild flowers that are so shy yet so colorful. It was miraculous how such gay things could grow under the shade of rocks and bloom into such color . . . such a riot of color that faced her in the doorway with Kunal's face just behind them.

She looked happy, thought Kunal, as happy as the

gulmohur tree had looked earlier this morning, and freshly emerged from some mental event of which he could be no part. The moment had come for one of their clashes—but it did not come. She was seeing him as part of a rock that glowed with warmth and color and he on his part thought she looked one with the miracle of the gulmohur tree. . . . And he had brought the flowers so late, so late because of a dead bird and a passing vagabond. The incident seemed to them both not annoying but humorous and they both burst out laughing. And so did the bird outside.

CHAPTER THREE

*A*nd far away in the school at Ispatpur, their second daughter so tuned to their moods sensed their laughter, and her wretchedness was eased a little. She was one of those children who cannot detach themselves from their parents and the shelter of their home. Had she been a fledgling sparrow it would have taken the united efforts of both parents to heave her over the side of the nest. Gargi, equally despairing over her and irritated by her, could not imagine how she would ever face boarding school later, or life in any of its myriad forms. She would stay at home always, Gargi feared, perpetually underfoot, and when her parents died she would develop into one of those old maids who have never left home. Gargi disliked old maids and felt that to be the mother of one would be the final humiliation in a life full of humiliations.

Kunal felt differently, for Pia was his favorite child. He was not irritated by her incompetence, her lack of confidence, or her present terror of everything that existed beyond her home, for in her he saw again the child he had once been himself. And he did not fear eventual loneliness for her, for he knew the preciousness of the single state. He thought he had chosen it once for himself—the books, the students, and the bare home. He had chosen it once, knowing it was the life for him, and then had come the ending of Gargi's engagement to some young blade in the city whom he had never met, and her despair, the despair of his young distant cousin whom he had loved all his life; and to serve her he had shut the door of the cell behind him with himself outside. He had lost his cell, yet it still existed somewhere within him. He believed that when he died, he would leave the cell to Pia as other men leave their daughters gold, money, or other material things. When she was old, she would go in and find peace. He did not fear for her old age, though he did worry about the stretch of time between now and then, for Pia had his temperament and he knew the burden of that.

He did not know her private joys, though he supposed she had them, just as he had. He did not know how his own awareness of beauty, his intense joy in it for a moment or two, and then his willing loss of joy, was in Pia an awareness of delight in others. She knew when people were happy, whether they laughed or not. Indeed, young as she was at eight, she knew already that laughter was not always a sign of happiness. Sometimes where people were completely quiet there came to her that wonderful sense of well-being, and her taut nerves relaxed in peace. But there was the other side of the picture. When others were wretched, no matter how well they hid it, she was anguished. She did not understand the reason for the deep alterations of mood that afflicted her and could not know yet of how acceptance of the change from well-being to its opposite, helped those who suffered. That supreme usefulness to which her awareness of the needs of others would eventually lead her was a long way in the future, and before she found the bare cell that she would inherit from her father, there would be a desert of ineffectiveness to cross, for she was one of those whose fear and reserve make it hard for them to have normal happy relations with fellow human beings.

But now, three miles away, a man and a woman laughed within the shelter of a campus sitting room, and though a minute ago her throat had been choked

with unshed tears, she was lifted by a wave of posi-
tiveness. She looked up bravely into the eyes of Miss
Bose. It was not so much because she had been
scathingly scolded minutes before that she was miserable, as because of the ugly wretchedness in the
mind of the woman before her.

It had created a miasma of hopelessness in the little classroom. The others had not felt it because
Miss Bose was unanimously hated and they got a kick
out of hating the bitch. Only Pia could not hate. She
went beyond cause and effect to reach into the cause
of the cause. But now the hopelessness was gone,
sucked up by the distant laughter like unhealthy va-
pors by the sun, and she looked up at Miss Bose and
smiled.

Her tormentor was checked in mid-torrent. This
was the first time that this meek child had stood up
to her; not in the obvious way that her older sister
did, with sarcasm and scorn or the younger one by
pretending the teacher was not there, but with tranquility. Miss Bose did not recognize tranquility but
found she could not go on tormenting her victim. As
well as tranquility some power of universal delight
came through the child Pia. ''Next one please,'' said
Miss Bose, putting the question to the nine-year-old
Rita. Rita answered it accurately, quickly, and con-

temptuously, her contempt being for Miss Bose's ill
temper, certainly not for her sister's ignorance.
How could adults forget themselves so? she seemed
to ask rhetorically. How can you teach children if
you don't have an understanding of little girls like
Pia? What had Pia and Gitashri learned at this
wretched school? She, Rita, had picked up a rich and
varied vocabulary that she dared not use and a
knowledge of the nasty ways of nasty women. She
also knew a great deal in the academic sense, but
this, she had learned from her textbooks and her father's books at home. She wished her parents would
take Pia and Gitashri away from Good Start. Good
Start, my foot! She had tried to tell Gargi once that
it wasn't a good school; they did not like it. Gargi
had said vaguely that of course no one liked school.
And it was exclusive. Did she want to go to the village school? Yes, she had replied cheekily. But Gargi
had stopped the conversation then. They were too
alike, mother and oldest daughter and in that lay a
danger. Father, of course, would listen carefully if
she told him, thought Rita, and instantly remove
them from Good Start. But that would be telling
tales, against Miss Bose and against her mother too.
And Rita could not tell tales. She had strong nerves,
a sturdy, thin body, and a stout heart. She also had

perfect understanding. She knew how much Pia suffered at the school but would never complain. Pia
also had her own brand of courage.

Rita sighed, withdrew a sticky sweet from her
pocket, and popped it into her mouth. She sucked
blissfully for a moment or two and then suffered a
pang of apprehension for it was a peppermint and
the aroma might possibly betray her. But she would
not take it out of her mouth. Only cowards went
back on things. People of spunk went on the chosen
course. She put her head down almost to her exercise book. She knew a great deal for her age but she
was unaware as yet that hot air travels upwards.

"Who is sucking a peppermint?" demanded Miss
Bose suddenly.

There was no answer for a moment until Rita
suddenly stood up, withdrew the offending sweet
from her mouth and held it aloft. "I can recommend
them, Miss," she announced, "ten paise at the station shop, Ispatpur terminus. . . ." Miss Bose shook
with anger, steadying herself against the wall. Her
head was worse today, the whole of her felt drained
and sicker than usual. She had been to doctor after
doctor. But no one was interested in nervous dys-
pepsia nor in an aging schoolteacher. Yet she had a

good brain and had passed Grade 8 at the piano when only fourteen. Had she been given a good training. . . . But no. Everything had been done for her brothers. And now look at them, wastrels both, and she a mere schoolteacher. Worse. A schoolteacher who did not like children. Job after bad job. If her father had left her one-tenth of the money he had squandered on the boys she might have bought a little house and had an annuity. She would not have to teach, or she would have administered a school and been happy. This was a bad school. Mrs. Zachariah was a bad schoolmistress. Faintness and nausea swept over Miss Bose and that horrid child Rita was holding a sweet right up to her. Beyond was the titter of the whole class.

"Go to Mrs. Zachariah," said Miss Bose.

For a girl like Rita, this was no punishment. She twirled her skimpy skirt with the same vivacity she imparted to everything she touched or wore and was gone. The titter stopped. Without Rita they were all afraid of Miss Bose. All except Gitashri who was angry and bored, sitting with the bigger children today as the kindergarten teacher, Miss Elizabeth Amos, was absent. Up went Gitashri's hand. She had had enough.

"May I be excused?"

"I suppose you won't return?" said Miss Bose with heavy sarcasm.

"No, I won't," said Gitashri lifting her lovely face. "No, I won't return today." She made straight for the dream world inside the curtained willow tree near the pond. She would not return today. Both her sisters had suffered. Now Miss Bose could suffer if she liked.

She did not know how long she stayed there until the voice of Miss Amos recalled her from Cinderella, Snow White, and Tom Thumb but she answered the voice in haste for she loved Miss Amos. She lifted the willow fronds and emerged straight into the arms of Miss Amos, hid her face against her linen skirt, and was happy.

But now here was Miss Bose approaching. "I will punish her, Miss Bose," promised Elizabeth Amos hotly. "She is a very naughty little girl." But her cheek was warm against Gitashri.

Miss Bose advanced a step, her thin hand outstretched. Elizabeth knew the feel of Miss Bose's hand, cold and clammy from ill health and to her vivid imagination somehow evil. She would not have it on the child. She swung away with revulsion, set Gitashri on her feet and ran, the child's hand in hers to the classroom where she taught the babies and Miss Bose heard the bolt shot in. Their feet had been light as summer rain pattering on leaves in a quick, unexpected shower. When they had gone the passage seemed like a tunnel from which all light had been sucked away. Miss Bose turned shakily into her own darkness and found that she was crying.

As she was not teaching until the next period, Elizabeth Amos's classroom was empty of everything, except fresh air, a potted azalea, and five little desks. Instinctively, ever since she had come to this school—in answer to an advertisement as well as the fact that it was in Ispatpur where her father worked as foreman in one of the surface mines— Elizabeth had fought its queer atmosphere of luxurious fugginess and bitter darkness with fresh air, bright colors, and cleanliness. Elizabeth lived in the school and went home on weekends. Her own room above her classroom, she had been able to furnish herself in flowered curtains and bright rugs of very little value. Her room was greatly different from those of her colleagues. Miss Bose's room was impeccably neat. The curtains drawn back from the windows as angrily and tightly as Miss Bose's own hair from her forehead. They were a slimy green, that green which is not worth calling green at all, so much is it the antithesis of freshness. It was a room full of hopelessness. Mrs. Zachariah's drawing room had rich brocade curtains of powder blue and vases of stale flowers unless parents were visiting. The windows were always closed. Against dust. But also against fresh air.

Elizabeth was a born fighter and it was because there was a battle raging here in this small school that she stayed, glorying in every inch gained here or there, a slackening of the forces on the other side. The other side? What exactly was the "other side"? It was a ridiculous and melodramatic way of putting it but still, Mrs. Zachariah was lazy and self-indulgent, Miss Bose sick and embittered. It was quite the wrong atmosphere for little girls to begin their lives in. That, so far as she knew, was all. Yet, the laziness of the one and the bitterness of the other seemed somehow a focus for more than themselves. Murkiness seemed to gather about them as bats and spiders are drawn to unclean and forgotten corners, and it was this negativeness that was a threat to the children. Elizabeth adored children and when she fought a battle for them she did so with more zest than usual. "Though what do I think I am?" she would ask herself during a rare wakeful night, "a rallying point for the hosts of heaven or what?" But this discouragement wouldn't last for long and she would carry on from where she had left off, teaching the children to speak the truth, keeping her temper with difficulty, being passionate in sympathy with the truly afflicted, remaining intolerant of malingerers, staying loyal to superiors, even if she hated them . . . All this and her only twenty years old.

Sitting in her chair, Gitashri standing before her, Elizabeth tried to sort out her thoughts and actions. What kind of punishment did this dreamy seven-year-old deserve? If she did the correct thing morally, Gitashri should go scot-free, but would she in future ever listen to Miss Bose? But the obstinate little girl never listened to Miss Bose anyway.

"You have been very naughty, Gitashri. Where have you been hiding?"

"I went to another country," said the child. "Have you never been there?"

"Another country? Who told you to go there?"

"I told myself."

Elizabeth laughed aloud. Shades of Maria Montessori. The oldest and the youngest of the Kushari children were difficult to punish. And Pia? She was her own punishment and would always be.

CHAPTER FOUR

*R*ita was still in the drawing room with
Mrs. Zachariah for Mama Zed, as all the children
spoke of her behind her back, had asked her to hold
her wool for her. As Mrs. Zed wound very slowly
indeed, and had a great deal of wool to wind, they
were still at it. Lazy though Mrs. Zed was, she did
knit. It was practically the only thing she did besides
eating and sleeping and reading love stories. Her
knitting was part of her pose; she was virtuous about
it. She was a very stout woman and had been a very
beautiful one. She had no idea at all that fifty years
and the addition of a great deal of weight to her originally slim figure had robbed her of her beauty, and
her conviction that she was still lovely enabled her
to retain the airs and graces, the self-assurance of a
consciously lovely woman. It also had its effect on
those who were with her. They tended to see her as

she saw herself. That is, for a short time. To see more of Mrs. Zachariah was to be less attracted to her. To see a great deal of her was not to be attracted at all. But there were few people who actively disliked her for they could not pin down what exactly it was about her that they disliked.

Thirty years ago she had married the solicitor for the Ispatpur mines, a man of some property and a great deal of standing. He had a large house by the river. She had been one of a large family of Armenians in a locality in central Calcutta tucked between Chowringhee Road and Chowringhee Lane.

There were so few Armenians left in the country that it was almost inevitable that she came to meet Mr. Samuel Zachariah on one of his many trips to Calcutta. As a young girl she had known hardship but she had all her wits about her. Mr. Zachariah was a sitting pigeon as far as Mama Zed was concerned, as well as an "open sesame." He was able to give her what she wanted and in return she graced his fine house and made herself agreeable to him personally with no dimunition of her smiling sweetness for four prosperous years. Then he died, leaving her the house by the river and just enough money. Stricken and lovely as a widow, she was for a short while utterly prostrated by her anger for she had expected a great deal more from her husband and had no intention of giving up the large house in which she had made herself very comfortable and which was a perfect background for her sweetness and elegance. She wept with rage in private and appeared in public most movingly pallid and heavy-eyed. So pathetic did she seem that all her husband's friends rallied around her and invested the money Samuel had left into profitable shareholdings for his widow. She did not want to marry again, for she had found even an indulgent husband exacting in his demands upon her body and attention. Also she had had one child, born dead, and she did not want to repeat a process that was disagreeable to her.

Looking for a way out of this dilemma it occurred to her to stay on in her house and open a small school for little girls in Ispatpur which could serve the children of the executives of the mines in the surrounding area as well as for many who lived within twenty-five miles of the radius around Ispatpur. It was true she disliked teaching, and indeed exertion of any kind, but if she could make a success of her venture she would be able to engage teachers from among the young girls in and around Ispatpur who had finished school and were waiting for marriage or jobs in a city. Everything worked according to plan; Mrs. Zachariah was a figure to inspire trust, and able businessmen and the gentry in and around Ispatpur entrusted their little girls to her. She remained comfortably off, in fact very well off. Good Start acquired an enviable reputation in the neighborhood of Ispatpur and after thirty years, even though it was declining both in numbers and prosperity, it still retained its name like the scent of old perfume in an unsettled wardrobe. Parents knew Good Start had nothing much to offer but Mrs Zachariah was "such a sweet person."

But the scent of a dying rose becomes at last tinged with the smell of decay, and so had the atmosphere of Good Start, emanating as it did from the extraordinarily strong yet lazy personality of Mrs. Zachariah. For beneath her sweetness and gentleness she had always been strong; in her youth this had been determined in appropriation, and now in her age it was just as determined in relinquishment. It was not easy to realize that strength could exist enclosed in such obesity and flabbiness, such laziness and self-indulgence, and hardly anyone did realize it apart from a few children, and their unconscious knowledge showed itself only in the form of a curious shrinking from Mama Zed's sweetness.

Even Elizabeth Amos, intuitive as she was, regarded Mrs. Zachariah as less dangerous to the children's well-being than Miss Bose with her cruel tongue.

Mrs. Zachariah's present state of torpor had not crept upon her unawares; it had been deliberately tilled by herself. This condition in which she merely sat while everything she wanted came to her without any effort on her part was what she had always wanted. Comfort had always been her god, and to achieve union with what she wanted she had, in her earlier days, been willing to work hard, heartily though she loathed work. Now it was no longer necessary. Opposite the armchair where she sat was a cabinet and on top of it a porcelain figure of the laughing buddha in all his smugness. She smiled at it.

"Thank you, dear," she said sweetly to Rita as they finished a skein and rested after their frightful exertions.

"Have another chocolate, darling, and give one more to James."

Rita gave one to the little Apso so unimaginatively called James and took one herself, because any chocolate is better than none. But she did not really like Mama Zed's chocolates. They never had hard insides and Rita liked confectionery with a good crunch to it or alternatively with good staying

power. These were squashy like the dispenser. The
room too was fussy and Rita had a sudden longing
for the cold austerity of her own home. Going
home, only a few hours away, seemed suddenly to
be at the other end of time.

"I do feel odd," she thought.

But mercifully her attention was distracted by a
knock on the door. Gitashri hovered in the doorway. Gitashri so disliked Mama Zed that it took all
the willpower she possessed to shut the door behind
her and advance to where the headmistress sat. Her
dislike dated to the day when she had been with
Mrs. Zachariah in the sitting-room and James had
brought in a field rat and tormented it upon the carpet and the headmistress had laughed.

"What have you done, dear?" asked Mrs. Zachariah languidly. She had no desire for an answer,
and Gitashri gave her none. All her pupils understood that her question was rhetorical and that she
would have been very annoyed if they had answered
her. Her staff sending her errant children was a nui-
sance, but at least it was an acceptance of and an ac-
knowledgement of her authority.

"Brush and comb James, Gitashri," she commanded.

Gitashri brushed and combed James with reluctance; she always thought of him as part of Mrs. Zachariah. In his obesity, his laziness, his indifference to the suffering of field rats, he was so very like his mistress that it was a natural conclusion to come to for a seven-year-old. But today, possessed as Gitashri was of the extra awareness that was always hers after she had visited that other country under the willow tree, James just seemed another creature with a miserable life, detached from Mrs. Zachariah.

Gitashri sat back on her heels and studied James. He was fat and unhealthy. His fur had not been trimmed during the last rains and the bangs of hair falling over his eyes almost blinded him. And he panted as no dog ought to pant. Now Kantak, her great-aunt's labrador, ran miles and then he panted. No, Aunt Kanan would not have liked James and neither would Mother. But was it James's fault? Mrs. Zachariah did not even seem to know that anything was wrong with her dog. Gitashri stroked one of James's ears with the brush gently and the dog snapped. She held on to its hot little body. Mrs. Zachariah's love for James was a sham, she decided. The woman did not even know that James had eczema. Suddenly she lifted the dog in her arms and ran out of the room.

"What is wrong with Gitashri?" inquired Mrs. Zachariah placidly of Rita.

"She was going to be sick," replied Rita.

"But she has taken James?"

"Only out into the garden," said Rita.

"Fetch him back at once," said Mrs. Zachariah. She showed no agitation for it was always too much trouble to show agitation. But James was her possession and he must be fetched back.

"Do as I tell you! At once!" said Mrs. Zachariah.

Outside, another, more frenetic, drama was going on. A sobbing Gitashri was surrounded by all the children and Miss Amos. "She shan't have him! He is ill. And she is so lazy she can't even look after him! I'm taking him home to Mother!"

James struggled. He liked Gitashri but the pressure of her little arms around him was too much. Also, arrayed against the child was a trio whose joint personalities were too strong for him. Mrs. Zachariah, Rita, and Miss Amos seemed all to be calling him; nay, demanding that he go inside again. He wriggled and leapt at Mrs. Zachariah. Pulling free, he went straight into the warm, powder blue room. "Bitch," screamed Gitashri, "you bloody bitch!"

Mrs. Zachariah merely smiled before turning into

her room again. And for the first time in her life
Elizabeth was thoroughly frightened of someone.

———

Elizabeth went into the kitchen to make tea for Miss
Bose. "Not that one fancies even a cup of tea out of
this kitchen," she thought in disgust, looking at the
greasy sink, the slovenly maidservant asleep in a
chair with her mouth open. Old Paulina. There was
a heap of unwashed saucepans piled in one corner.
Couldn't Paulina at least soak the dishes in hot water
and soap? "Cleanliness is next to godliness is an old
wives' saying, but there is a lot in it. It wouldn't surprise me," thought Elizabeth, "if one slid down to
hell, all the easier and quicker because the path was
slimy with grease, kitchen grease as well as grease of
an unwashed sin." The kettle came to the boil and
she was glad to have her thoughts deflected to Miss
Bose and her tea.

Kunal, so ashamed of the contemptible small battles in which his weakness daily involved him, would
have been encouraged if he could have seen the
strong-minded Elizabeth brought to a standstill outside Miss Bose's room with the tea-tray on a window sill and her hands over her face, while she
fought her detestable, detested, uncharitable loath-

ing of sickness in unattractive people. "You're hateful, woman. Aren't you a Roman Catholic?" she admonished herself, "you loathsome reptile, do you call yourself a human being and a Christian? Think of Christ—did he shrink from the lepers? Yes, but she's so ugly when she's sick. And so cruel to the children. Why can't Pia's parents see that she is being hurt daily? Once and for all Elizabeth, are you going to take that tea in or not? Very well then, hate her but go in to her or damn your soul in hell forever." Knock. "Please may I come in?"

There was no answer to her knock and she went in. After the heat of Paulina's kitchen, the stark cleanliness of Miss Bose's room came upon her with the shock of a cold douche and she was reproached by its extreme cleanliness. If she had gone to bed with a shocking headache she would have kicked off her shoes anywhere, dropped her clothes on the floor, and flung herself upon the pillows with complete abandon. But Miss Bose had folded her sari carefully, placed her shoes symmetrically and covered herself with a sheet. She had partly drawn her curtains and her room was dim. She lay with her face to the wall and gave no sign of recognition as Elizabeth came up to her and put the tray on her bedside table.

"Miss Bose, I've brought you some tea."

"I don't want it," said Miss Bose rudely.

"It will do you good," said Elizabeth. "Take an Anacin with it. My father always says Anacin and a Gelusil taken together with tea work wonders."

"Nothing does me any good," snapped Miss Bose. "Why can't you let me alone? Did I ask you to come fussing here? Take the tray away."

With her cheeks burning with shame and indignation, Elizabeth sat down on the bed. "What was the good of sending me in here?" she demanded silently of whoever it was. "Just look at us! We'll murder each other in a minute or two, and then where shall we be? But I'm damned if I'm going to be driven away by her vile temper. Here I'll sit till she takes an Anacin."

She sat looking round the room. It was so bare, so utterly unlike her own. No pretty things on the dressing table—not even a bowl of face powder. No photographs. Hadn't Miss Bose got a family? Didn't anybody ever give her a present? But how spotless the room was! "You couldn't say that of mine," thought Elizabeth, "I don't go in for all this spit and polish. Of the two of us, she is less likely to end up a slut like Paulina than I am. She's disciplined and I am not. I could be a slut. Yes, I could. I could be cruel too. I am. Look at me sitting here in a temper trying to force the wretch to drink tea that she does not want. Mary, Mother of God, have mercy upon all women, for all women are beasts underneath except only you, and I sometimes wonder about you too."

She got off the bed and picked up the tray. "I'm sorry," she said gently. "I'm going away and leaving you in peace. But I'm sorry."

Gasping with pain at the movement, Miss Bose turned over and opened her eyes. In the changed voice there was some compulsion that she was not about to disobey. It was Elizabeth's voice, yet it had in it a depth of compassion far beyond this Elizabeth's capacity. "I will do as you say," she murmured, and did not know to whom she spoke.

———

Astonished, Elizabeth put the tray down again, poured out a cup of tea, took two Anacin from a strip beside the bed, and helped Miss Bose to hold the cup while she drank and swallowed them. The tea was by this time lukewarm and Miss Bose had a moment of panic lest she be sick.

"Don't let me be sick," she prayed. She had not prayed for years and to whom was she praying now?

And what a ridiculous prayer! She shut her eyes, fighting down the nausea. Then she opened them again and found that Elizabeth was once more sitting on her bed. In the dim light of the room she could not see the girl's face very well, but she could see her dark chestnut hair, touched by a beam of light from the window. It looked like a plume of feathers. What was this brown-crested figure sitting on her bed? A bird of some kind? "Patience fills His crisp comb." Ridiculous, the way poets were always using birds as metaphors.

"I believe I am going to sleep," she murmured.

"That's the Anacin working," said Elizabeth. "I'll go now."

"Thank you for the tea," said Miss Bose, raising herself a little. She was not an attractive sight as she turned her face towards Elizabeth, with liver patches on her sallow skin and her straight grey hair in wisps about her face, but her bitter down-turned mouth had a suspicion of a smile about it, and Elizabeth smiled broadly back. Miss Bose's ugliness, and the rather aggressive health of Elizabeth's hearty smile, were veiled by the dimness of the room, so that neither felt repulsed. Instead each felt that strange movement of the spirit that can come when two strangers meet and know that they are no longer strangers. Elizabeth picked up the tray and went out of the room. As she went out, she heard the clock in the faraway convent striking the hour. "I always like to hear the clock strike," she thought. "It's one hour nearer the ending of life. A reminder. It's incredible that the seraph should bother about horrid women like me or Miss Bose."

———

There was a happy chirping in the passages as the children got ready to go home. Elizabeth, standing at the front door, thought they might have been sparrows, so loud was the chirping and so filled with satisfaction. Perhaps the purpose of sparrows, as of children let out of school, was just to remark loudly and with satisfaction and repletion that in spite of any appearances to the contrary everything was quite all right. If the repetition seemed a little monotonous at times, that was one's own fault; in a world where mynahs sing and willow trees became green-gold havens, boredom should have been included among the seven deadly sins.

Rita, Pia, and Gitashri were the last to leave because Gitashri had lost the rear end of a chocolate rabbit, which she thought had fallen out of her pocket in the passage somewhere. It took a long time to run it to earth under a table which, because Paulina never swept under tables, was very dusty. A dead spider had become attached to the rabbit and Gitashri carefully disengaged it. It was better to eat the rabbit straight away rather than lose it again was Gitashri's deadly logic.

"How patient Mrs. Kushari is today," thought Elizabeth for usually Gargi came in to fetch the children if she suspected them of dawdling. Elizabeth admired Gargi immensely. Rather blatantly pretty though she herself was, she envied Gargi her ethereal lightness, the beautiful worn face. Gargi looked like a tired moonbeam—without an ounce of patience.

It *was* surprising that she did not come in. But when they came out into the doorway it was not Gargi who was in the car but Kunal.

"Papa!" cried the three little girls in delight.

"Mummy could not leave the staff-room tea," explained Kunal. He opened the door of the car and got out, and Elizabeth, who had never seen him at close range before, watched in delight as his ramshackle length of limb emerged from the ramshackle contraption of a machine that was his car. Gargi's beauty tended to obliterate the charm of the old

Ford V8; one saw her and not it. But Mr. Kushari and the car were one, the one the perfect setting for the other. And though none was a beauty, they both seemed symmetrical and all of a symphony with the Ruprekha river, the tall sal trees beyond, the willow tree, the song of the birds, and Elizabeth's gay heart and love of life.

This sense of kinship with particular things and people was not new to Elizabeth. As one lived in a place, certain things about one—the branches of a tree seen through one's window, certain aspects of the light, a farm in the distance—moved forward from the rest of one's surroundings and became the furniture of one's private world. One could not part with that particular tree, that farm throbbing with activity without a sense of personal loss. And so with certain people. At some particular point in time a person perhaps known before, perhaps not known, would step forward from the teeming millions of the world, part the branches of the tree of life and come right in. "He has Pia's eyes," thought Elizabeth. "He is a better father than most."

"How do you do?" she said severely for she was always severe with parents. "I am Elizabeth Amos, Gitashri's class teacher." Then her severity vanished abruptly and she chuckled, ''There are only two classes, Miss Bose has the other. She teaches Rita and Pia.''

''I have not had the pleasure of meeting either of you,'' said Kunal with a humble courtesy that delighted Elizabeth again, ''but I have always known your father, Mr. Frank Amos.'' Elizabeth was a redhot radical and reveled in her lower middle-class background but she handed it to these landed Kusharis. They had something. They might drive battered cars of any vintage and wear ragged clothes but you knew them by the air of assurance with which they wore their rags, or paradoxically by the almost deprecating courtesy that was the outward sign of an inward grieving that they had been born one of the few and not one of the many with whom they communed in spirit.

''You have met Mrs. Zachariah?'' asked Elizabeth and discovered slightly to her surprise that she really wanted to know.

''Yes,'' said Kunal gently but briefly. Elizabeth looked at him attentively, for he was the first parent she had talked to who had not commented on Mama Zed's sweetness.

Elizabeth stood looking at the sal trees, and found

that Pia and Gitashri were on each side of her and that she was holding their hands rather tightly. Rita had already left them and was sitting in the car. That was as it should be, for Rita had already finished with Good Start and this meeting of parent and teacher did not concern her.

Elizabeth pressed the children's hands warmly for a moment and then released them. Unbeknownst to herself, she was standing straight as a spindle, which had always been her stance when facing something unpleasant. Kunal saw the attitude and smiled.

"Run and get into the car, girls," he said. After they had gone, he turned to her. "Something wrong?" he asked.

"It's Miss Bose," she said breathlessly. "She's not good for Pia."

"In what way?" asked Kunal sharply. At once he had become a different person, clever and penetrating. Elizabeth was glad of it. "She's a cruel woman. She is cruel to almost everyone but Pia is vulnerable so it hurts her the most."

"Have you an explanation?" snapped Kunal and Elizabeth realized that where his children were concerned he was as vulnerable as Pia.

"She's a sick woman. She suffers a great deal."

"From what disease?"

"None. Just dreadful headaches and so on. You know what I mean."

"Yes," said Kunal grimly. "And she retaliates."

"Retaliates?" asked Elizabeth, puzzled.

"No one helps her. In such circumstances it is natural to have a grudge against the callousness of the whole human race, and to avenge oneself upon such as are vulnerable. Unconscious perhaps. You and Miss Bose are friends?"

Elizabeth fancied sarcasm in his tone and was ashamed. Did he think she was one of those detestable women who delight in running down other women in the presence of men? Well, it didn't matter what he thought, but sudden anger made her face him squarely. "Yes. Until ten minutes ago I thought I hated her. Ten minutes ago we became friends." Looking at him she thought, "Strange. He is not sarcastic." She had been a fool to think he could be, for sarcasm does not grow on the same stalk as humility. He really wanted to know. She went on, "That sounds odd, I expect, but you know how it is. Someone you have known perhaps for years steps forward from the background and is suddenly inside with you."

"Yes," said Kunal and now there was the

warmth of amusement in his voice. "You like to be well understood, don't you? You like to have as many people as is possible in that mind-world of yours."

"Yes."

"You have done the right thing. Pia's happiness is of more importance than loyalties."

He touched her lightly on the shoulder, got into his car, and after many false starts finally took off. Elizabeth turned into the house. It had the kind of windows from behind which people peeped. It was a horrid house, she thought. But it needn't have been.

CHAPTER FIVE

"Well, why not?" thought Vikram, wandering northwards on the Mohurpukur road. Saved from hunger by the cut of his clothes and the benevolence of a Don Quixote of a landlord, he was able to look upon the world as a more promising place than he had been able to last night and earlier this morning. "I wish I could make a niche for myself in a country like this one, inhabited by Don Quixotes and the knights of Malory, a world of grey rivers and hillocks with lambs stuck all over their sides." He kicked angrily at a stone in the path. What was the good of fumbling after the magical experiences of childhood? They had vanished. What was with him now was the misery of going exhausted to bed and lying awake, dreading the years ahead, or waking from a nightmare and feeling the darkness lying on him with appalling weight and knowing that he

could never undo what he had done. Then the fear
could be sickening. "Ye know not when the master
of the house cometh, at even or at midnight or at the
cock crowing or in the morning." From what re-
cesses of his mind had that quotation come? The
master. What a name to give to those visitations of
the dark. Yet not unsuitable because for most men
in these times fear was the master of life. "Come
on," he said to himself, "this isn't these times. It is
another country where time has stood still without
stagnation. Come on, find the old lady with diamonds in her ears. Perhaps there will be peacocks
on her lawns as well."

Far above him the cranes were filling the sky with
their excitement. Vikram rounded the hill and saw
the Big House in front of him at the bottom of a
sloping field. He sat upon a log at the edge of the
field and stared at it. It was a stone house such as the
wealthier of Calcutta's residents built in the Chotanagpur belt for their holiday homes. It was quite
perfectly built in the shape of an E with tall chim-
neys and faced south across the river. The flat roof
had concrete balustrades interrupted every ten feet
or so by stone urns. The big porch, which formed
the central part of the E and most of the front of the
house, seemed to be covered with a wild white jas-

mine creeper. The leaves were a very dark green. From where he sat he could not see the back of the house, only imagine its wild beauty.

As he came nearer, Vikram became increasingly aware of dilapidation. His conjecture that the roses had not been pruned for a hundred years was going to prove correct. The japonica hedge had not been cut for many years either. The stems looked like brown sentinels wearing coral-colored headgear and the coral sprays tossed in the light wind. Three of the windows of the house that looked westwards had lost their small diamond panes of glass and been stuffed not with dirty rags or cardboard but with leather handbags filled with something or the other.

The field came right up to the house on the west and Vikram could not only get a good view of the handbags but also see into the lower room. It was a small library entirely lined with books. He gave an exclamation of pleasure. The old lady would have Cervantes there. She'd have Malory, Trollope, and Jane and all the writers in whom he delighted because they wrote of a world of people who did not live on the edge of a volcano, counting out the last minutes before it erupted; and whose laughter, while they did the waiting, set one's teeth on edge and drove one to do rotten things. "Don't make excuses," he said to himself, "you did rotten things because you are rotten."

He swung away from the window and walked on beside the japonica hedge that bordered the garden on the west, and was so overgrown with honeysuckle and impenetrable that he could see nothing either through it or over it. He imagined there would be a gate soon. There was. A low gate so overgrown with the same creeper that it looked as though it had never been opened. In fact the whole atmosphere of the Big House was like that in *Sleeping Beauty*. He did not want to disturb the atmosphere or the honeysuckle, so he climbed over the gate.

He surveyed the garden with amazement and delight. There appeared to be no one about and he could stare as he pleased. It had once been laid out in parterres of grass and flower-beds, and stone-paved paths with steps leading terrace by terrace down the slope to the river, and with a quick flicker of imaginative retrospection he saw it as it once had been. It must have looked like Tenniel's illustrations in *Alice in Wonderland*. For a moment he could smell the garden as it had been in those bygone days in the heat of a pre-summer sun.

The vision passed and he saw a grey day and such ruin that his delight turned to sadness. Yet still there was a scent of flowers, for as he moved forward he found clumps of small purple stock running riot over the edges of the weed-filled flower-beds and the moss-grown paths. There were drifts and pools of crocuses in the wild rough grass and the sweet briar hedges and the standard roses had flung out wild sprays of branches glowing with new leaves. The plants in the borders were not quite buried. A garden once given life struggles to maintain that life and here and there were signs that someone still cared.

Somewhere behind him upon one of the stone-flagged paths he heard the sounds of light, firm footsteps and the swishing of heavy silks such as could be made by a very old lady wearing very good silk. She was coming, like Maud into the garden. His heart was beating like a drum and as regularly. It was as if he was waiting for his lover. He was afraid to turn.

But turn he did, slowly and dramatically, ready to bow, and found himself confronting a fat, black baby calf. The shock was so great that he bowed to the calf. It was beautifully draped in a silk sheet and had no horns. "Vikram Sen, you are the most unutterable ass," he said aloud and bowed again. Then he looked with admiration at the calf's hooves tied with bows in soft felt. He bowed again. To his townbred wore her sari draped frontwards over her left shoulder. There were no diamonds in her ears but the sari was pinned to the blouse with a large diamond brooch. The brows were beautifully arched over her lovely eyes. Vikram knew at once that she had had great beauty: vital, compelling, and very sure of itself. He had meant to practice his charms upon this old lady, but instead he found himself hooked and landed by her own.

"Well now, young man, what is it?" she asked, and though the tones were sharp she seemed in no hurry. She belonged to a generation that had never hurried. "I am Kanan Kushari," she went on, "Kananbala Kushari." From a purse depending from her waist she took out a gold cigarette case, offered him one, and took one herself. As he lit hers and then his own, she watched him, not narrowly but with a benevolence that was both keen and gracious. In her day she must have been mistress to many servants, hostess to many guests. It had been her life to extract service and to give pleasure with equal competence.

"Sit down," she said, motioning with her cigarette towards the steps with, "if we sit on them, Vimla can't go down."

ignorance a calf was just a smelly cre
calf, this black beauty, was a revelation
can be.

"Don't let Vimla go down those st
voice and Vikram looked up to see the
old lady, dressed in silks, just like the c
towards him. "The slope is steep do
river," she continued, "remember the
swine?"

"I often do," Vikram called back, "I
devils. Have you a large herd? Of cattle I r
swine."

"No. Just Vimla. Someone gave her t
keep her well-dressed and exercise her. \
you by the way? Have you a message?"

"Yes," replied Vikram, "I've come to d
message and I'd come up to the house, only
seems anxious to go down the steps. What sh
do?"

"Stay where you are. I'll come to you. Th
you could shout the message. There's no one
but the plants. And they keep their secrets."

She walked slowly down towards him. She h
nut brown face and large expressive eyes. Her
was cropped close to her head and was a blu
white. Obviously great care was taken over it. !

She leaned back against one of the urns beside the steps and looked a question at him.

"Madame," he said, "I won't keep you. I have no message and I am trespassing."

"Why are you trespassing?"

"I was going to ask you to give me a job, as a gardener, a handyman, anything."

"Do you know anything about gardening?"

"Very little."

"Then why should I take you on?"

"I was not thinking of it from your point of view."

"And how were you thinking of it from your own?" she asked. "Did you by any chance think it would be a good place to get rid of those devils you spoke of?"

"That's exactly what I did think."

"My dear boy, devils are not so easy to get rid of as you think."

"I realize that."

"How long have you been in Mohurpukur?"

"Since this morning."

"Have you met my nephew, the professor?"

"Yes."

"Did he suggest that you come here?"

"No. The idea was mine. He told me of you. I don't know anything of gardening or anything else, but I could learn. I desperately need somewhere to stay. For a while . . ." he finished lamely.

"Where is your luggage?"

"I haven't any."

"Where did you spend last night?"

"On the train."

"And the night before?"

"In prison. My name is Vikram Sen."

"Sorry if I should have heard of it. I haven't. What were you in prison for?"

"It was thought I had killed my wife."

"And had you?"

"Not physically. But I created the circumstances that caused her to kill herself. Actually I was in prison for that."

"What saved you from the actual charge of murder?"

"I was on the landing of the flat below when the shot was fired."

"What do you feel now?"

"Shame and remorse."

"Shame and remorse are good things when they are your own." She held out her hand. "No, I am not saying good-bye. You may stay here. But can you fend for yourself? Cook a meal, wash up, make your bed?''

''Yes, I think so.''

''Then put Vimla into her room. It is down the back garden. And I must apologize to you. I was not brought up to ask questions.'' She got up to go into the house and turned round once to say, ''And welcome, Vikram.''

Devi Kananbala. So much charm. For a moment he wished with all his heart that she was young. Then he did not. Where would her deftness be then? Her wisdom and compassion? Like honey to the discarded helmet, these things come to their full glory only when the pride of life is past. She seemed to read his mind and smiled. ''I did not need that reassurance,'' she said.

CHAPTER SIX

*A*t the door of the cowman's lodge Kunal lifted his hand to knock and then dropped it again. Kishun wouldn't want him. What could he say to the old man that would be of the least use? What could he say to any one of his villagers to which they would ever pay the slightest attention? Other landlords coming as visitors to their lands from far away, could wear anonymity as a cloak of office, that was not without impressiveness if they did not stay too long, but he could not do that. The older among the villagers had known him in his weak and miserable childhood, his ineffectual boyhood and manhood. They knew all about the Kusharis and had told their children what they knew. No one would listen to him here. But then being what he was, he would never be listened to anywhere, and here he was at least in his own place. Here he could keep at least some sort of hold upon the very poor health, which was all he had ever attained to, and not fall sick as he did whenever he went to strange places. He decided to knock. As he knocked, his heart was beating faster than usual, but not so much with the habitual dread of making a fool of himself as with amazement and wonder at heaven's use of fools.

From inside came a surly growl. Kunal opened the door cautiously and stuck his foot inside, but there was no need for precaution. Kishun was obviously not well enough to shut the door in his face and Kunal's diffidence vanished in concern. He forgot himself and entered almost precipitately.

Kishun had been born and had lived in this little house for seventy-five years. His father who had been head gardener at the Big House had lived here for thirty years. Only Kishun, the youngest of his father's children, was left now and Kishun was Aunt Kanan's gardener, cowman, and general handyman. He gave to her the loyalty of a long line of devoted servants to a long line of devoted masters and mistresses.

This attitude on the part of both servant and master was peculiar and difficult to comprehend by those who were not of their generation. With far too much to do and far too little pay for the doing of it, Kishun was prepared to serve Aunt Kanan until he dropped. It had never occurred to him to do anything else. Now that his health had failed and he was old he could have been pensioned off but when Kunal had once suggested this course, old Kishun had only been able to master his fury by remembering that Kunal was a Kushari and also daft. He would have died for a Kushari as a matter of course and as casually as he cleaned out the cowshed. Yet he had no conscious appreciation of Kanan Kushari as a woman and was abominably rude to her at times. All he knew was that she was Kanan Devi of the Big House and he was Kishun of the cowman's lodge.

Miss Kushari on her part would never have thought of dismissing Kishun, no matter how rude he was or how incompetent. Had he taken to stealing, it would have made no difference. He had been a little boy at the lodge when she was a little girl at the Big House and she had never known life without him. Had it been necessary she would have given her life for him as casually as he would have given his for her, yet it never occurred to her that her calf was better housed than the man who looked after it and that she ought to do something about the unhealthy little lodge in which he lived and suffered the tortures of acute rheumatism.

It never occurred to her that Kishun might live in less pain were he to use one of the many unused rooms at the Big House. She had the softest of hearts but to her Kishun and the lodge were inseparable. Everything had its allotted place in Mohurpukur, like jewels in a crown, and to move anything from where it had always been would have seemed to her an act of sacrilege. Kunal however did think of it, but Kishun's language when he had once suggested removal to the Big House had been such that from then on he had kept his thoughts to himself. Old Kishun in his lodge was like a snail in its shell. Dug out of it he would now be more ill than he was in it, as Kunal himself was when separated from Mohurpukur.

"You there, Kishun?" he asked unnecessarily, feeling himself into the darkness of the room. He crashed into a rickety bamboo table.

"Careful now, Kunal Babu, you clumsy—" Kishun bit off the word without speaking it. He had always been able to do that even before Kunal became an adult. For the poor dolt was, after all, a Kushari.

"I'm sorry, Kishun," Kunal said. "How bad are the pains? Is it the screws again?"

"Screws and the stomach," and Kishun embarked upon a long history of his illness while Kunal actually listened. When Kishun's privacy was invaded he was like a snarling animal surprised in his lair, but once he adjusted to the interruption the instinct of the animal gave way to the gregariousness of the country man. But that was all he did. He made no appeal. Patience was the basic fact in his pain. His narrative was like a flower sprung up out of the rock of resignation; the flower soon withered but the rock remained.

Finishing his narrative, Kishun sighed and the sigh caused him to belch slightly.

"Pardon," he said with grave, sad dignity.

"What a fool I am!" ejaculated Kunal, "I am entirely forgetting what I came for," and he produced Vidya's little flask.

"Thank you, thank you, sir, Kunal Babu, Professor!" Kishun was so touched that the various titles by which Kunal was known fell off his lips. "That will set me up fine and you need not trouble to walk uphill again, Kunal Babu."

"But I will, I will," replied Kunal.

Vidya deserved a medal, many medals, he thought to himself as he stumbled out of the lodge. She always knew what was best for everybody. Without that brandy, his visit to Kishun would have been a fiasco, an absolute fiasco!

––––––––

"Now I'm here I must go and see Aunt Kanan,"
thought Kunal as he trudged further uphill. "But I
must hurry or Gargi might be upset if I'm late for
dinner."

As he toiled uphill he suddenly remembered that
the man he had met on the road this morning had
drunk most of the brandy. Fool! Ass! Criminal fool!
Shame seized him, abysmal shame and bitterness.
He had little sense of proportion and all his failings
ranked as crimes in his eyes. He turned and ran
down the hill again but before he reached Kishun's
door he stopped, halted miserably and uncertainly,
and then turned back up the hill once more. For
what was the good? How could he explain what had
happened? It was such a mixed-up story; he could
never hope to disentangle it. Poor Kishun would be
both hurt and annoyed.

Inside the lodge, Kishun was having the laugh of
his life. Poor Kunal Baba. He must have put the flask
down somewhere and someone had finished half the
contents. The fool would never learn! He stopped
laughing and thought back with infinite tenderness.
Just like that time; it hardly seemed such a long
while ago.

Kishun had decided he must have a birthday just like everyone in the Big House did. Kunal, seven or eight years old at that time, had saved up his pocket money and bought him a packet of cigarettes. On his way through the kitchen garden to the back regions to present them he had remembered that he had forgotten to feed the then puppy of the house. He had put the cigarettes under a bush while he ran back to the kitchen. Some hours later when he remembered, the packet had been half emptied by a gardening helper. Poor little Kunal, how he had cried. But Kishun had tweaked his ear and said that the half-packet of cigarettes was worth more to him than a diamond from the queen of England. "He won't change, always the same," thought Kishun again, and from the cowman that was the highest praise.

———

Walking in the dusk to the front of the house, Kunal was surprised to see the shaded lights on in Aunt Kanan's dining room. She usually had her evening meal very early for she had no servants except old Kishun. Visitors. Kunal turned hastily away, for he hated visitors, either his own or other peoples'. He was aware of the inconsistency but nevertheless he

loved beings and hated visitors. His definition of visitors was narrow: no one lacking this world's goods
was a visitor. No one sick or in any trouble or perplexity was a visitor. No one very old or very young
was a visitor. In fact what it boiled down to was that
he was terrified of well-dressed, confident, trouble-
free people who called for no reason other than the
social. He was not inhospitable but he was wary of
small chitchat.

"And yet you are a Kushari," Aunt Kanan had
said once. "Our family has always had such nice,
easy manners. Your father could be charming even
in his cups and your lovely mother had manners to
match her face. Why go so far? Just look at your
Aunt Vidya's manners. Charming!"

"It is my house," thought Kunal now, "whose
honor my aunt Kanan is upholding. It would have
fallen to ruin long ago if she were not in charge. The
way the world is going we shall not have this house
or the college much longer. The college is struggling
along on subsidies. I have begged them at the university to make it a constituent college. But all they
have done is to affiliate it. Now if only Aunt Kanan
could go to the university top brass, she could make
them do whatever she asked. . . ."

Kunal opened the door to the hall of the house

and walked in. Kanan Devi's reaction to him was what it had always been: mingled affection, pity, and exasperation, exasperation predominating. He was a Kushari and a good man as all the Kusharis had been. His childhood had been pitiable, and she had not done all she might at that time to make it less so and for that she reproached herself now, but it tried her sorely that such a poor, weak creature should be the only man left to them and should have no sons . . . though for that she blamed Gargi who had made only three attempts and then desisted for reasons of finance. Finance! In her young days a little thing like finance never deterred a woman from carrying on with the duties of her state . . . now she must stop thinking of Gargi, an irksome subject, and attend to the matter in hand.

"Vikram, I think you have already met my nephew. Kunal, Mr. Sen is paying me a visit."

Vikram flushed and got to his feet. In the old days he could have carried it off; now, in this house he could not. "Mr. Kushari, Professor, I did not quite plot this. But I needed a place to live. Please believe that."

All his natural ease had deserted him. He stumbled over the spate of words. It was Kunal who was at ease now. "You are welcome. Aunt Kanan's guest is my guest."

They sat around the dining table in perfect ease. Aunt Kanan's labrador, Kantak, came up to be patted and introduced. It was a lovely time in a lovely house and they talked in harmony of this and that. The evening flew by, the dog had fallen asleep and Kunal suddenly realized that Gargi would be waiting the evening meal for him.

"Aunt Kanan, did I telephone Gargi?"

"Not that I know of. Why?"

"To tell her I am here."

"Was she expecting you at home?"

"I rather think she was."

"Then you had better go home at once," said Aunt Kanan soberly.

It was over. The charmed circle vanished, and though the door was still shut, the windows closed, all at once the wind seemed to be in the room. Kunal got up, put his arm around his aunt and hugged her. He patted Kantak and smiled at Vikram. But all the time his eyes were sad with self-knowledge. He opened the front door quickly and was gone.

"I like to sleep early," Miss Kushari said. "Leave

the dishes on the table, Vikram. We can wash up in the morning. Take a good book to bed.''

''Just one moment, Miss Kushari.''

''Yes?''

''Who is Gargi?''

''Kunal's wife. Why?''

''I used to know a Gargi.''

''She wouldn't be the same one,'' said Kanan Devi firmly. ''Good night.''

''Good night and thank you.''

ikram chose *David Copperfield* from the library and half an hour later was in bed with it, but time went by and though he had the book open he could not concentrate on it.

One fear, among many others that had dogged him always, was the fear of poverty and passing now in thought through the gamut of his fears he remembered the day of its inception. He had no memory of his parents; he had always lived with his maternal grandmother and had been ten when she had died but even now he could never smell eau de cologne without revulsion because her room had smelled of it on the day when he and Mr. Mitra, the lawyer, had sat one on each side of the table with the ink-stained cover while Mr. Mitra explained that his grandmother had not been clever about money and so now there was nothing left for him. The kindness of distant relatives would provide for his school days and food and shelter in the holidays, but after that he must fend for himself. He must work very hard at school, and he must be very clever and do very well, for he would have only himself to depend on when he left school. Mr. Mitra had meant well but he had explained himself badly. He had made that which had awaited Vikram seem like a black pool of horror into which he was to be tipped headlong in only eight years' time. Vikram had gazed at the largest inkstain (he had stared at the inkstains on the table throughout Mr. Mitra's monologue) while Mr. Mitra talked and it had got blacker and larger as he gazed. It was destitution into which he would fall when his schooldays ended. . . . For he knew very well that he could neither work very hard nor be very clever. A boarding school was sought and found for him but the other boys laughed at him because of his stutter and his lonesome ways and the fact that he was no good either at his studies or at games. His refuge was the shed at the end of the garden where he scribbled stories of great horror and revenge against his tormentors. He could find relief nowhere except in that shed.

The blots of ink had got smaller and less enduring as time passed and he had grown tougher. He had grown out of his stammer and had developed good looks, vivacity, and charm, and a brilliance of imagination that had tricked all but the most discerning into thinking that he was a good deal cleverer than he actually was. But he did not trick himself and the fear of poverty had been with him all through life and had brought him to the ultimate disaster.

He had written plays for a living and his name was known, at least in a few discerning circles. His late wife, Keya, belonged in these circles and was rich and as ambitious for him as he himself was. She was a follower of the rising sun. But all that apart she was, first and foremost, rich. They married and it was disastrous—a life of parallel solitudes, acrimony, and utter lack of communication. Keya was highly strung and he had failed to see her needs. Until that fateful afternoon.

It seemed as if they could have no dialogue without the words turning into drops of poison. And before long Vikram had taken to not answering Keya at all.

"I'll kill myself!" she had screamed.

"Go ahead," he had replied and walked out of their apartment down one flight of stairs to the landing below. He was staring miserably down the stairwell when the shot had rung out, metallic and

ominous. He'd turned and run up again. Keya was
lying sprawled in the sitting room. The face was un-
touched but there had been nothing left of the back
of her head. She had done a thorough job of dying.
Later he was told that she had put the nozzle of the
revolver into her mouth and angled it backwards.
Under Section 306 of the Indian Penal Code, Vikram was sentenced to two years' imprisonment; it
could have been far worse. . . . Ever since then he
had dreamed that Keya was at his bedroom window,
wet, with huge droplets of water running down
from her eyelashes. My God! To be able to sleep
without dreams! Tonight he was drifting into a light
sleep and he thought, "Why, Keya, you are not outside anymore. . . ."

———

In her own room downstairs Miss Kushari was sitting up in her large bed. She had a shawl around her
shoulders and was adding up lists of figures with the
help of her account book and passbook. Her face in
the dim light looked haggard and old. She was badly
in debt. Even with the allowance Kunal gave her she
was in a very bad way. She put the books on her bedside table, turned out the light and lay down but not
to sleep. She lay facing the window, looking out at

the moon. She had slept in this room since she was sixteen years old, and she was now eighty-two. She was wedded to this house and could not leave it. Things were undoubtedly in a bad way, but she would contrive to manage them somehow as she had always contrived. She would write to Narayan Singh, her lawyer, who was also good at contriving. They had been in many tight places before but they had always managed by selling land or jewels or liquidating out investments. It was unthinkable that she should leave the Big House and it was not hers to sell. It had been just as unthinkable that she should have left Kewal, her brother (who had lived in the Big House during his lifetime), and Kunal's father, and fortunately, Kewal's wife had thought so too. "My sister will live with us," Kewal had told his wife. "But naturally," the lovely young bride had replied. The two things—her brother and this house—had been the abiding passions of her life.

Kunal had often suggested that the Big House be given over along with the college to the Department of Education. He had suggested that a little house be built for his aunt next door to his own cottage but the thought was loathsome to his aunt. There would be Gargi to play second fiddle to, she thought, and as an afterthought, "I am not yet a humble woman."

After Kunal had finished his studies in Calcutta he had come back to Mohurpukur to run the college that his grandfather had founded and financed. He would not live in the Big House. Besides he had just got engaged to his young cousin, Gargi, and he hoped his aunt Kushari would be pleased. Kanan was far from pleased. She had not seen Gargi for years but she remembered her as a remote and self-willed child. More recently Gargi had been in Calcutta and had got engaged to a city man, the bohemian kind, so Kanan had heard. The engagement did not last and now she was going to marry Kunal. Kanan in great distress of mind foresaw no happiness for either.

She was not sure how it had worked out; not very happily she imagined but somehow better than she expected. One thing was sure. Gargi resented her and it was mutual. But in old age, how it all fades away. She did not care if Gargi even hated her. It would be a compliment actually. But it would still fade away. Disconnected thoughts passed through her mind. Gargi's pride, her own willfullness. That young man upstairs, what had he done? If she gave in to Kunal and the Big House was taken over by the government, wouldn't it be all for the good? She drifted towards sleep and thought that white feath-

ers were falling on her face and that a swan was singing. The music was familiar and just as she was trying to remember where she had heard it she fell
asleep.

CHAPTER EIGHT

*T*he morning dawned calm and lovely. From her bed Vidya could see the hills beyond the river, the woods, and the sky. Like all those who spend much of their life in one room, she had come to have a personal love for her window. She slept with the curtains drawn back, and whenever she woke in the night she looked towards it eagerly to see what it had to show her: the clouds like galleons crossing the face of the moon, gems of stars set in a pall of black velvet, Aurora like a golden lamp above the brown rim of a dawn sky. Once she had woken up at dawn, she did not often go to sleep again, for her window faced east and she could not bear to miss a moment of the sun's rising. She loved to see the distant woods, grey and colorless while Aurora still blazed, dressing themselves in color as the starlight faded. Above all she loved the dawn skies with their alterations of bright beauty, flaming so quickly to the penultimate splendor then passing from glory to glory until the colors were lost in the opening of the full day that her eyes could not catch the moment of change; in the span of a breath one glory had passed and another was passing and she could not hold the moments as they came. Perhaps only she was awake in all of Mohurpukur to tell of what had been. Yet how could she tell? That was what bothered her.

She would say to Gargi, "It was a lovely dawn today, so full of color," and Gargi would answer, "Was it, Vidya? Could you manage meat for lunch or would you rather have an egg?"

And she would say, "Egg, dear Gargi," and think how lopsided were the gifts of God. Now why give a woman eyes to see and no words to tell of it? The way Nature squandered herself was criminal! The longer she lived the more deeply aware did she become of profundities of meaning in everything about her.

She was roused from her reverie by Kunal bringing her an early morning cup of tea. Winter and summer alike he entered her room scrupulously shaved and meticulously dressed at 6:30, carrying her tea. He might have all the trouble in the world keeping his mind to the point, controlling his nerves

and emotions, but at least he had now got his early
morning routine running on rails. He leapt from his
bed as soon as his alarm clock rang at 5:45, stifling it
promptly lest Gargi in the next room be disturbed,
stumbled in a state of trembling misery to the bathroom, and took a cold bath to the accompaniment of
"Jana Gana Mana," which he intoned with groan-
ings and croakings like a frog in a swamp. His bath
over, his misery hardened to a resolute and solid depression and he dressed and shaved in silence as for
the scaffold. That done he made Vidya's cup of tea
but did not have one himself, considering it contrary
to discipline. But he made her cup of tea extremely
well, exactly as she liked it, for at this time of day he
was so focused upon the ideal of perfection that he
could scarcely go wrong. There were no distractions
yet. No one yet would tell him that the equipment
in the psychology department was out of date or
there was a shortfall of five thousand rupees for the
class two staff's salary. Therefore there was no
major problem to plunge him into despair. He did
not take much notice of Vidya at this time of the day
unless she were unwell, but kept his greetings and
inquiries until later. He merely satisfied himself that
all was well with her, wrapped her shawl around

her, delivered the tea, and went out again, for he kept silence before breakfast.

Drinking her tea, the best she would have in the whole day, Vidya knew Kunal would go to his office in the college complex, go over his accounts, perhaps feel happy that so many of his ex-students had offered to do voluntary teaching at his college while they decided what they wanted to do in life.

When she finished her tea Vidya lay back against the pillows and tasted the flavor of the day. She always had a shrewd idea as to what sort of a day it was going to be like at the cottage, and adjusted herself beforehand to storms or peace. Yesterday had been on the whole a good day. After what had seemed a dangerous start with the flowers for the staff room, Kunal and Gargi had seemed in harmony with each other and the children had come back from school happy. But their parents had not ended their day happily. Kunal had forgotten to come back to dinner; Gargi was proudly silent and this coldness had lain on Vidya's heart like a stone. Alas! she thought, it takes a happy marriage to make light of small things. But what was the root of their unhappiness?

Gargi, she suspected, could uncover the root and

air it if she tried, for roots can be ugly things. "One of these days," thought Vidya with mounting exasperation, "I'll make her." Then she controlled her exasperation and put the thought from her. She did not believe in forcing anything, in having things out; things came out by themselves with patience and goodwill. She comforted herself by looking out of the window, for undoubtedly she knew it was going to be a difficult day. Her fingertips pricked with the knowledge.

———

His pen in hand, ink all over his fingers, Kunal looked down at his lecture notes in despair. He was no teacher. The very glory of the things he wanted to say seemed to get in the way of his saying it. Try as he might, he could not speak about what he knew. How do you tell a class of youth the rightness of the fact that Christmas Day used to be celebrated by the Babylonians a hundred years before Christ was born? And why? He was like a man trying to catch the moonlight on the water with a fishing net. When he pulled the net into his boat there was nothing in it except two repulsive jellyfish and a bit of seaweed. Had he ever had doubts about his knowledge, had he ever had to hold it at arm's length and argue about

it, words might have come more easily. He put his
notes away in his desk now and knew a peace that
would last until he had to mount the rostrum and
stumble through his pitiful dissection of the two jellyfish and his bit of seaweed.

His mind was distracted by other worries, pri-
marily the problem of that poor, wretched elderly
teacher and Pia. The chief worry was Pia but there
was Miss Bose too. It might be that her need of rescue was greater than Pia's. He couldn't think what
to do about it. Time and time again he dragged his
mind off Pia only to have it circling round his cow-
ardice in not braving Gargi's displeasure and bringing Vikram to his home yesterday. It had turned out
all right, for Aunt Kanan had made good his deficiency. If he had done his duty he would not have
ended up having dinner at the Big House, for then
Vikram would have been with him and he would not
have wounded Gargi so cruelly by forgetting to
come home in time but he was back to square one,
Gargi would not have stood for the stranger in her
busy home; she had enough to do as it was. But the
forgetfulness! The knot had been in his handkerchief
all right, placed there when she had told him there
was something special for dinner, but he had
thought it was to remember to order the coal,

"which I haven't done even now," he thought hastily, and ordered it on a scrap of college notepaper. Then leaving his desk in disorder, he went to find Gargi, a more urgent problem at this moment than even Pia, for Gargi in one of her icy moods would cast a blight over the children's weekend. Usually when he tried to make things better between him and Gargi, he only made them worse, but he had to try.

Gargi was ironing.

"Why on a Saturday?" he asked her.

"I can't leave the whole lot till Monday," she snapped, "I washed out Vidya's messy tray-cloth and the children's blouses after dinner last night when you were at the Big House."

Her iron glided over the tray-cloth that he had forgotten to ask Rampujari to wash and he felt as though it were burning his soul. "I'm sorry, Gargi."

"What for?" enquired Gargi coldly.

"For all my deficiencies, but chiefly because we cannot afford to have someone to do the everyday washing and ironing."

"Which we could do if you would bestir yourself," said Gargi. "Lack of means is a deficiency which you could make good if you would only try."

vain. Her first lover had taught it to her and then had rejected her. When she had turned to Kunal she had found no assuagement. She had thought her own ardor was dead, but just now it came alive in a confusion of two men. Then suddenly the man was gone and she was clinging to Kunal in an abyss of humiliation. She laughed a little, uncertain of herself.

"Not the tangkas," she said. "Pia loves them and I don't really mind ironing. Anyway how exaggerated you are! Those tangkas will buy us the earth. They belong in a monastery or a house like the Big House with a separate Oriental room. And I like ironing. Really." After a while she added, "It was just that I was in a shocking bad temper."

"Not anymore?"

"No. Get back to your notes and I'll finish the ironing. The children's clothes must be done by Monday." He went, a little cast down by his dismissal. It was always like that. Just when they seemed to be coming closer together, she became a shadow he could not catch. And who had won the argument? Gargi, of course. Pia would be going to school on Monday.

———

Rampujari left early on Saturdays and so the family ate around the kitchen table in order to save labor.

"Has Vidya got her lunch?" asked Kunal, hovering over his chair in the shape of a bent pin.

"I took it up," said Gargi with a touch of sharpness. Kunal's habit of sloping upstairs on any excuse to Vidya tried her patience.

"You could fetch the tray down again after," said Rita cheekily.

Kunal lowered himself into his chair and smiled at her indulgently. She was an impudent little piece of goods, but she was angelic to look at and was very like Gargi at the same age, only Gargi had been a remote little creature and Rita was very forthcoming.

"Papa, you haven't heard a word," Rita reproached him. He had been vaguely aware of the music of her voice and Gitashri's in a duet upon the subject of Minnie the frog who lived in the vegetable garden. Apparently she had produced a string of jellied babies for all of whom names would be required.

"Tina, Mina, Anju, Manju, Madhu . . ." said Kunal instantly, "Ajay, Vijay, Pramod, Tom, Jerry. . . ." There were times when he could leap out of his customary abstraction with startling suddenness and be thoroughly focused, and he was so now, leaning his arms on the table and consulting earnestly with an equally earnest Gitashri. Their mutual earnestness about the creatures was their only likeness. The consultation finished, he leaned back and smiled at Gargi. All was well today with these happy children. And Pia?

Because he loved her the best, Kunal always looked at her last. Though she liked most creatures, she had a horror of the ones of the occult, bats and owls, toads and spiders, snakes and even cats. On her fingers she was counting up the number of toads soon to be at large in the garden. Her head was bent and her straight hair fell forward, shadowing her pale face. Her green frock had shrunk and lost color in the wash and clung to her sadly, like a cloak of drying seaweed about a stranded mermaid. She was, Kunal thought suddenly, exactly like the little mermaid in Hans Andersen's story, "a singular child, very sad and thoughtful." She never cried either. "Mermaids cannot weep, and therefore, when they are troubled, suffer infinitely more than human beings do."

"Don't count on your fingers, Pia," said Gargi sharply. For Pia it was a terrible reminder of Monday when there would be school again, school and arithmetic and Miss Bose. She looked up quickly, her face stricken, then braced her shoulders with habitual courage and smiled at Gargi. It was Kunal's smile, apologetic and deprecating; and like his it always annoyed Gargi, making her feel vaguely reproached when her intentions had been for the best.

"I do it too," whispered Kunal, slipping his hand under the table and moving his fingers on her lap to show what he meant. It was perhaps disloyal to Gargi, but the others were talking again and only Pia could hear him. He was glad he had thought of that mermaid who had followed the prince on bleeding feet. "All will I risk to win him and an immortal soul,"—a reading of Hans Andersen would help him to help Pia. She looked up and smiled at him, and he was reassured, as always, by the serenity of her eyes.

"What are you going to do this morning?" he asked her, for he knew she would not be engrossed with the toads like the others, "can you put my tangkas into order chronologically?"

She nodded, her eyes bright. "In your study? While you talk to Vidya?"

"Yes," he replied. "This child of mine explains and completes me," he thought as he went upstairs after settling her with his precious paintings.

———

He had meant to chat briefly to Vidya upon trivial subjects but old habits die hard and he had burst out soon after settling down, "That damn school!"

"I always suspected it was a damn school," said Vidya placidly. "Now sit down and sit back for goodness' sake and get it off your chest so that we can have some peace."

He leaned back, leaned forward again, then leaned back finally and poured the whole thing out.

"That poor woman," said Vidya when he had finished. "But it's not her that's the trouble in that school."

"Elizabeth Amos is a sensible girl and she thinks so."

"Sensible she may be, but at that age they never know as much as they think they do. It's that Mrs. Zachariah. I've never liked her."

"You've never even seen her, Vidya."

"Yes. But I've known of her. When you see the results, where's the need for seeing her? The language Rita uses! And the dirt at that place is shocking. Rampujari's niece works there and she says Mrs. Zachariah is a slut. Hardly ever leaves her bed. Our Rita, she's sharp, she's taught herself. But Pia, who is so full of imagination, should have done better.''

"She's too frightened to learn anything. Too terrified of Miss Bose.''

"And what sort of a headmistress keeps cruel teachers?''

"I expect she doesn't know, Vidya.''

"And what sort of a headmistress is it who doesn't know what's going on? That woman's no good. I've known of her since she came to these parts. There's cruelty, and bad language and dirt growing out of her. Let herself go, that's what she's done.''

"But what are we going to do, Vidya?''

"Have you consulted Gargi?''

"Not yet.''

"Then don't. If you do she'll go straight over to Ispatpur in a rage and get that poor woman dismissed.''

"Wouldn't that be a good thing?''

"Not for Miss Bose.''

"It's Pia I am thinking about.''

But Vidya had not finished with Miss Bose. "She cannot be a bad woman or that Frank Amos's daughter would not like her. Miss Bose would make a better headmistress than Mrs. Zachariah I don't doubt.

If she had a little more scope, trust put in her, she'd maybe turn out well. Why don't you go and see her?''

''Go and see her? What would I say to her?''

''How should I know?'' snapped Vidya, ''something or the other will occur to you. In the meantime, tell Pia that you know about Miss Bose and give her the choice of going back to school on Monday or not.''

''Vidya, why didn't you tell me or Gargi about the dirt?''

''And what would you have done on third-hand evidence?''

''Poor Pia! And she never cries. She's a child who feels intensely.''

''Is it the non-criers who feel most?''

''Yes. Don't you remember Hans Andersen's little mermaid?''

''I never liked that story. I don't hold with people trying to better themselves. We should all keep to where we belong. That mermaid should have remained in the sea, tail and all. And Pia should stick to the school until the end of the term so that whatever decision be taken, it is taken after consideration.''

''Should I speak to Pia now?''

"Yes, now."

Kunal picked up Vidya's lunch tray and went.

———

He entered his study and sat down. Pia did not look up from her sorting. As each tangka was placed on the other, according to the various stages of the Buddha's life, she proceeded to roll them up, three to each roll.

"Pia," said her father directly, "I am in a fix about your Miss Bose."

"Miss Bose?" Pia gasped and went rigid. "My Miss Bose?"

"Yes, yours. Your class teacher; I've been told she loses her temper with some of the children and makes them unhappy."

"Who told you?" Pia whispered, a white line around her mouth.

"Someone. Not Rita." Pia said nothing and he went on: "Now that won't do. Because it is bad for children to be frightened and unhappy. They can't pass exams that way. The only thing for me to do, I think, don't you, is to tell Mrs. Zachariah and get her to send Miss Bose away?"

"You can't get her sent away just for me. Where would she go? And not many of the children are afraid of her. Anyway one of the girls told me, Miss Bose didn't pass many exams and no other school would take her. She was also unhappy at home with her brothers so she had to come here.''

''It's complicated what you are saying. But the gist of it is that Miss Bose has nowhere else to go. Is that it?''

''Yes. I think she was ill the other day. She'd put her head on the table and was making hurt sounds; like crying but not exactly crying.''

''I know. Your poor Miss Bose. It must have been colic. Unkind people around her and an unkind body. Is no one kind to Miss Bose?''

''Miss Amos is. But not the other children.''

''Why not? Have they all got bad health or just colic?''

''What's colic?''

''A peculiarly painful form of indigestion. Makes you hate the world. That's why I thought the whole school must have colic except Miss Amos.''

''I don't think so,'' said Pia.

''Then I am at a loss to understand why everyone is so unkind to Miss Bose.''

''But they are not unkind, Papa. They are just not kind.''

''You must be one thing or the other. Do you

ever put flowers on Miss Bose's desk?''

"No, never.''

"Try doing that. People blossom if others are kind to them. But first, would you like to stay at home for the rest of this week? And next term after Easter would you like to go to some other school?''

Pia looked at him with incredulous joy. But her head went down again and there was silence.

"I'll go back on Monday. I can't just leave . . . just leave things half done.''

"Sure?''

"Sure.''

"My Chameli! My Chameli of the undiscovered woods, growing bravely! Now let's get on with the 'Songs of Milarepa.' '' And they both knew that a measure of their burdens had been lifted.

CHAPTER NINE

On Saturdays after tea Gargi always read to the children in the drawing room, and if he could, Kunal came and listened too. He came today and sat in the armchair opposite his wife. Gargi was not one of those women who kept their drawing rooms for special occasions only; she loved it and used it well, and enclosed in its beauty felt at rest and happy. For she had got this room as she wanted it. Nothing else in her life had worked out but this room had. It had been part of Kunal's wedding gift to her. Whenever she felt bitter towards her husband, she remembered the fireplace surrounded by smooth stones from the river bed, the Chinese lacquer cabinet, the Empire day bed, and the Kashmiri walnut wood sofas and tables.

The cottage was, officially or traditionally, the residence of the principal of the college. Before

Kunal, it had always been occupied by people who were not members of the family. It was only during Kunal's principalship that it became the residence of a Kushari while Aunt Kanan lived on at the Big House. When Kunal had become engaged to Gargi, he had tried to visualize her in the cottage drawing room as it was then and failed entirely. He had one wall wrenched off and the furniture discarded. For the first time in his life, taking no notice of Aunt Kanan's displeasure, he had ransacked the Big House for the most delicate pieces of furniture he could find and installed them in the cottage drawing room. The wall was replaced by French windows and that done, he had stopped, leaving the soft furnishings and carpeting, the ornamentation, to Gargi's infallible taste. She had done it with pride and joy, covering the floor with an oyster-colored carpet and hanging oyster-colored satin-cotton curtains at the windows. On the satin-cotton were forests of fuchsias with proud parakeets sitting on the branches of stylized trees. When the curtains were drawn, the room gave the effect of a dream forest. Japanese prints of flowers hung on the walls and the whole was rounded off with a few pieces of toffee-colored jade cups and books.

The children loved the room. Their mother was not quite the same mother in this as in the other rooms of the house. On the threshold of this room she seemed to shed her worries, to become younger and more beautiful, more loving and at the same time more remote and mysterious.

And the books she read to them here were also something apart. The schoolgirls' stories beloved by Rita were banned in this room. She read them Hans Christian Andersen, Charles and Mary Lamb, *The Secret Garden,* and *Puck of Pooks Hill.* "The best thing in the family week," thought Kunal, watching her as she read, "and today is better than usual. Today is best of all." He lay back in his chair and abandoned himself to the perfection of this gift. Five o'clock and a fine March evening.

"One evening, just as the sun was setting with unusual brilliance," read Gargi, "a flock of large and beautiful birds rose from out of the brushwood; the Duckling had never seen anything so beautiful before; their plumage was of a dazzling white, and they had long slender necks. They were swans. . . ." The dazzling plumage of the swans enclosed Kunal; he was a small sad boy again but uplifted by the words and the imagery.

"They uttered a singular cry," read Gargi, "spread out their long splendid wings and flew away from . . ."

The telephone rang in the hall. Gargi stopped short in her reading, and pulling his legs in abruptly, Kunal suffered a sudden stab of pain in the lumbar muscles. Rita said "Damn!" and Gitashri most surprisingly burst into tears. Gargi's and Kunal's eyes met and there passed between them a wordless message of fear. The telephone continued to ring. The perfect hour had ended almost as soon as it had begun.

"I'll go," said Rita, "it's probably Aunt Kanan."

"Rita's language!" mourned Gargi when she had gone. "Gitashri, what are you crying about?"

"It was dark," sobbed Gitashri, "and there were nightingales singing. Now they have all gone and there is light."

"You've never heard a nightingale, Gitashri," said Kunal, "they don't sing in these parts."

"Mine do," said Gitashri.

"You were asleep, Gitashri," said Gargi.

"I wasn't," replied Gitashri crossly, starting to bawl again.

The swan sang in the light, thought Kunal, and

touched Gitashri's cheek. "Okay, I believe you," he said.

Rita came back. "It's some man who's staying with Aunt Kanan. She's got more vegetables than she knows what to do with and wants to know if you would like some because if so he'll bring them down."

"So have I got more vegetables than I know what to do with," said Gargi quickly. "Say thank you very much but I won't deprive Aunt Kanan."

"I've said thank you very much and rung off," said Rita. "He's bringing a basket down."

"Rita, I've told you not to ring off before bringing me the message. And you don't like vegetables," said Gargi peevishly.

"I like men," said Rita simply.

Kunal sighed. The idea that in the upbringing of Rita the worst was yet to come had often occurred to him before. Then he brightened. "It's the man I told you about, Gargi. I'd like you to meet him."

"I've not the least wish to meet him," said Gargi as crossly as Gitashri. And then, "We were just beginning to enjoy ourselves."

"Then let's go on enjoying ourselves until he comes," said Kunal. "Let's finish *The Ugly Duckling*."

"You finish it," said Gargi, passing the book across. "I don't feel like it anymore."

She leaned back in her chair and Kunal went on with the story. He read aloud well, and though the perfection of the hour was shattered, the perfection of the story did not fail to take hold of them again. At the end the children were laughing and talking so loudly that Vikram, finding the doorbell out of order, could not make his knocking heard. During the last twenty-four hours such a measure of self-respect had been restored to him that instead of putting the basket of vegetables down in the porch and going away again, he opened the door and went into the hall. He saw the line of light showing under the drawing-room door and heard the children's voices and a wave of nostalgia came over him, not for his own childhood that had so soon become unhappy, but for the days when he had been a welcome guest in many homes. So often had he arrived unannounced like this, crossed so many halls and opened so many doors, that without being conscious of what he was doing, he did exactly that before remembering his mental picture of Kunal's shrewish wife.

It was too late.

His apologies were cut short by the beauty of the room and then by the beauty of the slight woman who first rose rather languidly to greet him and then stood extremely still, one hand at her throat, the other clenched at her side. The little silence lengthened rather painfully.

He had forgotten how small and slender she was. Over a pair of black pants, she wore a pink loose coat of Chinese brocade that suited the little air of arrogance and unapproachability she had always had. She wore her long thick hair as she had always worn it, swept back from her forehead and pinned at the nape of her neck. It was of a rare kind of black that had a Titian glow to it against any light and he had seen it and her face so many times in his dreams, the dark eyes and the small perfect features, the lovely mouth so unaccountably lacking in generosity, the rather hollow cheeks. What detestable luck, what damnable awful luck for both of them. Couldn't you ever do a thing and be done with it in this world? Could you never come to a new bit of road and not have the past running along behind the hedge on either side, mocking you?

She was coming towards him, the charming, noncommittal smile of the practiced hostess on her lips. She was speaking clear words of welcome and introducing her children. Her voice was the same. They had moved for long in the same world, he and she, and had made a fine art of dissimulation. Nothing had betrayed her but that momentary stillness. Only he knew that the beads of sweat on his forehead had not been brought there by the exertions of walking.

They sat down and talked for a while of trivial things, the burden of the conversation being sustained by Gargi and Vikram. Kunal leaned back in his chair and felt satisfied, it was so seldom that Gargi took to anyone. Vikram too was spilling charm. He seemed more of a man of the world today and Gargi was, of course, city bred. He felt an intense sympathy for this stranger. Thank heavens Aunt Kanan had asked him to stay. Thank heavens Vikram would have the time to remedy his damaged nerves. In a pause in the conversation Gargi said, ''I'll show you the garden; Kunal is reading to the children.''

They walked across the lawn and stood together by the briar hedge, looking out over the valley to the river and the hills beyond. The night was beginning to lower and the sky and river met in a wash of molten silver. Vikram felt he stood knee-deep in a liquid of that metal, and the silver letting through every gradation of soft color. He had to go from here just

as he had started to mend, he thought, and the sorrow was so bitter that he stood in silence and could
not say what he must say. Gargi waited, her body
lightly and beautifully poised, like a bird's just
before it took flight. Her face was expressionless and
yet in the very lack of expression, there was a hint of
cruelty. She did not hate the man beside her; she
was simply emptied of all human kindness.

For more years than she cared to remember there
had been this bandage of wretchedness on her eyes:
sometimes she was on another plane altogether, so
deep and engrossing was her personal unhappiness.

Upstairs at her open window Vidya watched
them. She had seen Vikram come and had thought,
"Must be the man staying with Kanan. Older than I
thought. He's seen too much. I'd rather be myself
than him for all that his body gives him no trouble."
Her quick sympathy had reached out to him. And
her delight too. It was grand to see a body like that,
moving so smoothly and painlessly, with such delightful ease. There was beauty in healthy bodies.

And now as she watched, it was the beauty of the
two bodies that enthralled her. To her fancy, had the
wind blown, they would have swayed and come together. Vidya looked more intently and her first delight changed to apprehension. She had never seen a

man and a woman who physically looked more fitted to stand together, and yet who were so not in accord. The very fitness of the outward picture gave cruel emphasis to a bitterness within; it brought tears to her eyes and a constriction to her throat. The endurance of so much pain had brought to her the same sort of awareness of the happiness or unhappiness of others that Pia had already as her birthright. Pia had been born a *Manushagan;* Vidya had received her sensitiveness as the alms of age, one that had refused to feed on itself. If it were a doubtful blessing, it was not the curse that absorption in self would have been. In the last resort there are only the two pains, of redemption and damnation, to choose from. And there was nothing she could do. Though the man stood, rooted and held in silver light as it were, her intuition told her he was being swept away. It was as if she herself were being swept down into a terrible vortex. And though the fragile, pink-robed woman could have put out a hand and held him where he was, she was incapable of that one small gesture of kindness. How many queens had made it! Just one small gesture of the hand and the life was spared. "You silly old woman," said Vidya to herself. "It's likely that the man has come about the insurance," but still she fell to praying. There was never any harm in being on the safe side. Not knowing that Vidya suffered way up in her room, Gargi and Vikram talked in the garden.

"Gargi, I'm sorry," he said, "I'll go of course."

"Of course," she answered. "And so you do not know Kunal and I lived here?"

She hated herself for asking the question, but she had so hoped when she had married Kunal only a month after Vikram had left her, that he would see the notice of her marriage and be humiliated to see how little she cared.

"No," he said, "I did not know you had married. I was in England."

Even in England, she thought, he could have kept himself informed of her well-being through mutual friends, if he had wished. She took her revenge with a charming politeness. "And are you famous now? Do you still write?"

He looked at her so compellingly that she had to answer his gaze though she had not meant to flatter him with so much interest. Even his lips were white. Had she hurt him as much as all that? She was delighted if she had but heavens, the vanity of men! She looked at him trying to think of something else to say that would hurt his pride, but he forestalled her.

"Gargi, do you really not know what has happened to me lately?"

"My apologies," she said. "I did not even know if you were alive or dead."

She spoke as contemptuously as she could, and watched to see his face tauten still more at the flick of the lash. Instead of that it softened and a little color came back. He smiled and his whole body relaxed with relief. She realized with a pang that she had not hurt him. He was glad that she had refused all knowledge of him since they parted. It was she who was suffering from hurt pride, not he. It made her feel at a disadvantage. She did not know now what revenge to take.

He turned away from her and spoke with gentle humility. "I am so glad that you live in this paradise of a place. I am so glad that you have married this very great man."

She was astonished. Mohurpukur? Kunal? It was not in this way that she had ever thought of either of them. Vikram stuck his hands savagely in his pockets as a small boy might do, and the memory stabbed at her. She had not forgotten a single of his gestures. He had always done that when he was deeply moved. Nervy, emotional creature that he was, his hands would tremble at the slightest provocation, and ashamed, he would hide them. He had always lost his heart very suddenly to places and people. He did not want to leave Mohurpukur. He did not want to leave Kunal. Nor would Kunal want him to go. Kunal, this morning, had said he liked him, had thought he needed help. Was that true? It might be, for Kunal had a nose for people in trouble. Her thoughts raced. To drive Vikram from his paradise, to deprive him of Kunal's friendship—that would be a revenge that would satisfy her. Her thoughts stopped with a jolt for one hand had come out of his pocket, and still trembling, held her arm. "I am glad I came though," he said. "I am glad I know how safe you are. It's such a beastly, terrifying world out-side."

She looked at him and the fear in his eyes shocked her. What a child he was! Did she think this because of the maternity that was now in her, or because of his faint, but to her eyes unmistakable, likeness to Rita?

How it had shamed her when she had first noticed in Kunal's child that fugitive likeness to the man she had not seen for two years. It had proved that say what they would, the intense absorption of the mind can influence even the physical likeness of a child.

He had haunted her like a ghost night and day. The obsession had not left her until Rita's birth and therefore she did not love Rita as a mother should love her firstborn. So disinterested was she that when Kunal asked her what name the child should have, she had answered vaguely, "Rita."

Now she fought hard, her longing to hurt at war with her sudden pang of pity, and then suddenly, through the intensity of her feeling she was aware of the silver light that was pouring over them. Its amazing beauty was like a voice speaking, a challenge like that of the flowers in the staffroom to her power of correspondence, and she could not react to it with the ugliness of refusal.

"Stay if you like," she said coldly. "Kunal likes you."

"Thank you, Gargi. I'd like to stay. I need to stay."

From within came the sounds of the girls' voices. "Mummy, we're starting another story. *The Princess and the Pea*," shouted Rita.

"That pea," thought Gargi. "It's just like Vikram. However many layers of oblivion I spread over him, he always comes through."

CHAPTER TEN

*E*lizabeth Amos woke up on Monday morning in a shocking temper. Then came the realization that it was raining, that it was Monday morning and that the string of underclothes she had hung up to dry the previous night in the bathroom was still wet and that she hated everybody. As a general rule her temper was of the firework variety, an affair of sparks and flashes that seemed a mere effervescence of her vitality and was enjoyed by all, but upon rare occasions she woke up in the morning possessed by an absolute demon. She could feel him flexing his muscles within her.

Yesterday she had spent most of her time in the Roman Catholic church in Ispatpur, praying a great deal for Miss Bose. By bedtime she had been exhausted by her own spate of words to the Virgin Mary. And today she had intended to inaugurate a new epoch at Good Start, an era of Christian charity which should gradually win each soul in the house to love first Elizabeth Amos, and then that way of life of which throughout yesterday she had been a shining example. She had intended to begin with Miss Bose, whose alarm clock was now shrilling in the next room.

"Damn that woman!" Elizabeth reached for her bedroom slipper and flung it at the partitioning wall. Mercifully it went wide off the mark, sending a vase of flowers on the dressing table crashing to the floor. She got one eye open properly and looked at the stream of water trickling towards a wide crack in the floor. Mama Zed's drawing room was underneath. Elizabeth smiled in unholy glee and beneath it her conscience nagged. "Damn that water!" She flung her bath towel savagely into the center of the pool and stood shivering in her dainty voile nightdress, looking irritably about her. By the time she had gone to bed last night her virtue had been wearing a little thin, and her room presented its usual morning-af-ter-the-night-before appearance. Every drawer and cupboard was open showing the confusion within.

For a moment she was aware of herself in her customary optimistic early morning manner, Eliza Amos, young, pretty and charming, and made a half

turn towards the glass to greet this nymph and para-
gon. She was met with a scowl, and glowered back
in return at the horror in the glass. It was too much.
A chastened appearance had to be her armor in the
warfare against the demon; it was also a sign to those
about her to take shelter. Just then the breakfast
gong sounded.

Brown seemed to be the order of the day, a
brown frock with a white collar and belt. Just as she
was brushing her hair Paulina knocked on the door.

"Didn't you hear the gong?" she asked.

"Of course I heard it," flamed Elizabeth. "You
sound that gong as if it were the last trump. And
what is it when you get there? Tepid tea and leathery
omelettes. I'd sell my soul to the devil that's in me
for the sizzling bacon and tomatoes you just took in
to Mrs. Zachariah."

Paulina, when she could summon the energy,
could also lose her temper.

"And who are you, Miss, to teach me my duty?
Do I carry on with the children's fathers in the
driveway for the whole of Ispatpur to see me?"

"So you've been telling tales about me, have you?
What a slithy tove you are!"

The allusion was lost on Paulina who had never
read *Alice* and could barely sign her name but she

recognized the tone of insult. She was furious but suddenly she started to weep. "God knows," she thought, "I could be angry like this vital young girl too but where did my downfall begin?" She sobbed.

Elizabeth, all amazement, thrust a dainty lace-edged handkerchief into her hands and said, "Cry, cry more and stop when you realize what lethargy has done to you." And with that she ran downstairs.

But worse was to follow. It was just one of those days. At the breakfast table she accepted her plate of cold omelette with a martyred air.

"Are you all right?" asked Miss Bose.

"No, I'm not," she snapped.

How old and yellow Miss Bose looked in the harsh morning light. Was it possible that only last Friday she had felt faint stirrings of friendship towards her? Was it possible that only yesterday she had thought that she loved the children? Silence reigned except for the champing of jaws and the clicking of Miss Bose's badly fitted false teeth.

"Now I know why language was invented," Elizabeth said to Miss Bose.

"Why?"

"To disguise the noise people make when they eat."

Miss Bose flushed. She was aware of the bad fit of

"But not by a man. There are lots of ways of being crossed in love."

"Really?" said Mrs. Zachariah. "I am always delighted to learn."

Again aware of the sarcasm, Elizabeth yet stood her ground. "One is in love with life when one is young," she said, "one trusts it. I expect Miss Bose did. And now look at her, after it's let her down."

"I look at her every day," said Mrs. Zachariah, "and see a woman in a most enviable position— easy work, a comfortable home, and good food."

"You know nothing about our food," flashed Elizabeth, "and you don't care. That's what makes Good Start such a vile institution—that you don't care. Just look at James, for example, you keep him just like a dog—a pet; you don't care about him as a person."

"A person! Elizabeth, you people of mixed blood are so exaggerated. No sense of proportion at all."

Elizabeth turned and ran out of the room. Had she stayed she might have murdered Mrs Zachariah.

———

Mrs. Zachariah lay back on her pillows trembling with the violence of her anger. Fear and anger, the two enemies had come upon her by stealth and thrown her. As a girl she had had something of a temper but had subdued it with the immense strength of her will, realizing that cold, clearheaded calculation was a more valuable instrument for ambition. Once she had reached maturity nothing had made her angry except her husband's death. It was inconvenient; it was fearful. She had dealt with fear. Nothing was more inhibiting than fear, nothing more confusing to the judgement. Yet here she was, thrown into a panic by a silly girl's defiance. For just a moment there had opened up before her an abyss of intolerable emptiness. Her comfort had momentarily seemed not a hard-won Utopia that would never know change but a facade erected to hide that sharp brink beyond which there is nothingness. She had never thought of the fact of death in relation to herself. She had of course never wanted to, and never tried to, and having never loved she had never known the bitterness of death. Her husband's death had disturbed her only from the material point of view. But Elizabeth's defiance had caused her to question her own sense of security. She was holding the reins of an institution—but what was the point of it if she were doing a bad job of it? If there was no achievement, there was no security. The smooth succession of her comfortable days was only a stream carrying her to the brink. She looked at the fat little dog on her bed. A lapdog had seemed a necessary element in her comfort, a sort of extension of herself upon whom to lavish the caresses and indulgences of self-love. Now for the first time she saw what a repulsive object the little creature had become under this treatment and with sudden energy she kicked him off the bed. He fell with a yelp to the floor and lay there stunned with hurt astonishment.

Mrs. Zachariah lay back against her pillows again, furious, exasperated, and afraid. Not for years had she put forth so much energy. She was panting and for the first time in her life she felt ill, not just indisposed but deathly ill. Terror such as she had never known, terror to which her past fear had been a mere nothing, rose up before her like a black wave, before crashing down and blotting her out.

Yet presently she was lying in her bed as usual. She would have said that she had gone down screaming, that the room had fallen into ruins about her, but there was no one with her and the room looked just as before. Her sight seemed a little misted and she realized that she had been blotted out for only a short while . . . blotted out. The phrase was full of horror for her. ''Blot his name out of the book of life.'' She did not know where she had heard that sentence, but as it came sliding into her mind she felt sheeted with cold. The iciness was creeping up from her feet and when it reached her heart she would die. ''I must have a hot water bottle,'' she mumbled. ''Quick, quick, Paulina, a hot water bottle or I'll die.''

But Paulina was not there and when she tried to lift her right hand to the bell, she could not move it. She lay there for a full ten minutes, breathing heavily, the sweat of her agony breaking out on her forehead. Not physical agony for she felt no pain, but the agony of her realization. Then she tried again with her left hand, found she had the use of it, reached across her immense self and rang the bell. Presently Paulina was beside her wiping her hands on a greasy hand towel. ''Get me a hot water bottle, Paulina,'' she whispered thickly. The mist had cleared from her eyes now and she could guess what she looked like by the expression on Paulina's face.

''Why, Madame, you do look poorly,'' Paulina said in surprise. ''Shall I get the doctor?''

''No. A hot water bottle.''

''Best you get the doctor,'' pleaded Paulina.

''No,'' said Mrs. Zachariah.

Even now her will could compel and Paulina ran.

"I'll never sleep," thought Mrs. Zachariah, "never sleep, I'll never sleep." But mercifully as the warmth stole up her body she began to feel sleepy. When she was deeply asleep, snoring heavily with her mouth open, James knew there was no more hope for him to be reconciled with his mistress and he crept from under the bed and dragged himself through the open door. Outside he paused. His ear hurt him badly. He trembled in pain and loneliness. The door of a cupboard across the landing was open and he went morosely towards it. He crept into the darkest corner and lay there still trembling.

———

Miss Bose, in her pristine bedroom, stretched the counterpane over the bed she had just finished making and glanced at her watch. Every morning now she had to fight a desperate reluctance to take up the burden of the day. The weight of her despair was at its worst in the mornings. As the day went on, it got a bit easier, but at first it did not seem possible to face those children again. She hated them! Especially that angelic-faced Pia Kushari, whose defenselessness aroused all the cruelty in her. She was dimly aware that she was cruel, but she seemed as powerless to control the rush of sharp words to her tongue as she was powerless to control the onset of pain in her body. Both seemed to have their roots in her exhaustion, that deep soul-exhaustion of which she was aware but did not understand. But she knew it was a vicious circle. The harder she fought her pain and her cruelty the more tired she was, and the more exhausted she was, the more ill and bad-tempered she became.

Once again her first lesson that morning was arithmetic. Of the various lessons she taught, arithmetic was the most agonizing to her and her pupils. Yet in her own school days maths had been, after music, her favorite subject.

She remembered she had even been brilliant at it. The precision of it, the infinite variety within the framework of eternal and lovely law, had roused her awe and delight in much the same way as music had done, and the sight of the stars on a clear night. There, too, in the glory of the night sky the law was inviolable. The music of the spheres. The dancing measure of words in great verse. The song of the birds, obedient to the swing of the seasons and the dawning or waning of light. In her youth she had never thought of the divine marriage of order with infinite variety without longing to feel the pulse of the dancing measure in her blood, aching to hear the unheard music.

Crossing the hall to the classroom, she was astonished to find that she still remembered how she had once felt about these things. There had been a freak March rain and she stopped in the hall and noticed how the mist of the rain was thinning and the light breaking through. Outside the window sprays of a rose tree hung low, heavy with the rain, and each spray was strung with silver drops. What was happening to her that her eyes should be opened like this? What was happening to the house, that its atmosphere should be freshening about her? It was as though far off across a waste of mud flats the bright tide had turned.

She opened the door of her classroom and went in. The rows of detestable little girls were demurely yet rebelliously seated behind their ugly little desks. She felt, as always, their hatred rising against her, forgot the bright tide and hated them in return. She was aware again of that dull, muffled feeling in her head, the precursor of a more violent headache, and of a gripping pain below her breasts. Desolation seized her, and the sharp words that she would use presently thrust through it like steel needles in her mind. She walked erect to her desk and heard in anticipation, shrinking from it, the dull thud that the pile of exercise books would make when she dropped them on the hard wood.

But she did not drop them. She stood holding them, gazing at the bunch of brocade marigolds on her desk; rich maroon and speckled with yellow. They had been painstakingly arranged, yet with a sweet, wild grace that delighted her. She put the exercise books down very gently and picked the flowers up. Their pungent smell was in her nostrils and the wet of the rain on her hands. She lifted the bunch to her face and was carried back forty years to the Burdwan village where she had gone to stay with her grandparents, a thin-faced town child whom no one had cared about. But she, in those days, had cared about marigolds, wet moss, and rain.

She looked up and saw all the little girls watching, wondering how she would react to this unprecedented occasion; all but one staring at her with mockery, curiosity, or dislike, but nothing else. The one exception was Pia Kushari at the end of the row, who was gazing at her with an expression of pure pleasure. She and Pia looked at each other and between them was spring.

"Thank you, Pia," said Miss Bose. "Now who will fetch a vase of water to keep them fresh?"

Every child in the room put up her hand. This was a grand arithmetic lesson. Five minutes of it gone already and another ten before the flowers were arranged. "Gitashri," said Miss Bose, "you fetch it." She chose Gitashri because a few minutes ago the curiosity on the child's face had borne no likeness to the curiosity on the faces of the others. The rest had been wondering which of several possible reactions they would have the pleasure of tearing to tatters during the break, but Gitashri had been merely wondering what expressions of pleasure would fall from Miss Bose's lips when she saw the flowers.

Miss Bose looked again at Pia. Was I such a child, she wondered. Did I have that expressive face? And it's been my pleasure to torment her? What have I become? A new sort of pang wrung her, the first of its kind. It was as though a hand suddenly squeezed her heart, so that she was breathless. And she was supposed to be giving an arithmetic lesson.

"Isn't it March the twenty-first?" she asked her astonished class.

"Yes, Miss Bose," replied Rita promptly.

"The first day of official spring, if there is such a thing in this country. We shall read a story today. A story about gardens."

The class was flabbergasted.

"Rita, fetch *The Secret Garden* from the bookshelf, will you?"

Gitashri came back full of importance, gingerly carrying a water-filled bowl. Her Miss Amos was still with Mama Zed and she sat down to listen to Miss Bose who was reading. "There were other trees in the garden, and one of the things which made the place look strangest and loveliest was that climbing roses had run . . ."

CHAPTER ELEVEN

"**M**iss Amos, I'm worried about Mrs. Zachariah," said Paulina. "She's sleeping so heavy."

"I don't doubt it," said Elizabeth with heavy sarcasm. It was lost on Paulina. "No doubt you cooked her an excellent lunch?"

"Just some grilled fish and cauliflower cheese. But she didn't eat it."

"Really! People don't eat when they sleep, you know."

"I wish you'd just step up and take a look at her, Miss," pleaded Paulina.

Elizabeth had reached the front door during the course of this conversation and she said desperately, "It's my half day off. Anyway, I'm no good at illness. Ask Miss Bose if you are really anxious." And she turned and ran. She did not stop running until she was some way down the road. Even then she walked quickly with a queer feeling in her spine, as if she expected a fat pudgy arm to reach out and draw her back to Good Start. The sensation is well known by those who have only one half-day off a week.

As she came to the Crooked Bridge, a faint gleam of sun shone through the rain and lit the wet granite to silver. The fugitive moment of beauty came down like a bright sword between Elizabeth and Good Start. When it passed, she was set free.

She stood at the parapet and blinked at the water, which was now liquid silver. The sun was out again. She turned, conscious suddenly of someone with her, not just passing by but with her as no one had been with her yet. A tall figure, haggardly handsome with sad, troubled eyes.

"Please forgive me, but could you tell me where the vet lives?"

"Which vet? There are two. One for cats and dogs. And the other for sheep and cattle. They both do both but they are specialists."

"Cows," said the man. "One calf to be precise. Vimla."

"Vimla? But that's Miss Kushari's! My father

gave her to her. Gave Vimla to Miss Kushari, I mean.''

They started to walk together towards Dr. Das's. She suited her stride to his, contentedly and easily, walking not as people walk in town, going a short distance in a hurry, but as they walk in the country, going a long way for pleasure. Standing beside her he had been with her as no one had been with her. Just asking for guidance he had said something profound; walking together she could scarcely believe that five minutes ago she was alone. What was happening? So when it happened suddenly, this was how it happened! The magazines had got it all wrong. And today, with the demon raging within her she had not even bothered to wear makeup.

''It's that house over there,'' she said, ''the one with the brown door.''

''Have you had lunch?'' he asked.

''Are you asking me to? Because if you are, there are no places to have it in this village.''

''There is,'' he said. ''The *dhaba*.''

She hesitated, for once in her life at a loss as to what to do.

''Have you a name?'' she asked, ''or shall I call you Vimla's fetcher-of-the-vet?''

"Just let me finish with the vet and I'll tell you," he answered.

He wasn't long and they retraced their steps across Crooked Bridge. "My name is Vikram Sen," he said, "and I am working as Miss Kushari's cowman and everything else. She's most extraordinary. She didn't blink when she heard I'd been in prison."

Elizabeth didn't either. They reached the *dhaba* and ordered a rich, indigestible meal. "You haven't told me who you are," Vikram said.

"Elizabeth Amos. I teach Miss Kushari's nieces."

"Do you? I've met them. I like Pia the best."

They ate their meal with relish and Vikram paid. His bank now had instructions to send him money to Mohurpukur. All in all, he was a happy man, for the moment at any rate. Suddenly, as they were walking back, Elizabeth asked, "Why did you tell me you had been in prison?"

"Because no one can be expected to build a friendship in a vacuum," said Vikram, smiling. "There must be a few facts to make some sort of scaffolding." He paused and she could feel by the unease in her own body how difficult it was for him to go on. Then he plunged jerkily and curtly into it. "I had a profession. Actually two. A writer and the husband of a very rich woman; you're bound to love one more than the other and sacrifice one to the other. And that's what I did. My wife committed suicide and I was imprisoned for two years for aiding and abetting it.''

''I remember now,'' said Elizabeth. ''I read about your trial and I've read two of your books.''

''Did you like my books?''

''No.''

''Do you like me?''

''Rather.''

''Well, here we are, back at the bridge. You go across it don't you? I stay this side.''

He had had enough. That ''rather'' was said in an offhand way as if the last hour had not mattered at all. He was abrupt with his good-bye but she did not seem to mind. He stood and looked after her. My thoughts are going after her, and it is that way my soul would follow her, lightly, airily, and happily and I would be rid of all my great troubles, he thought wretchedly. For, of course, it was something that would never be.

CHAPTER TWELVE

*G*itashri had inherited not only her father's love of creatures but also his knight-errantry. From when she was very young she had been fishing spiders out of ponds, putting moths out of the window and placing creatures that had got upside down the right way up again. She was ever on the watch for those unfortunates who had fallen into, or been placed in an environment unsuited to them, and no consideration of personal safety or convenience were ever allowed to stand in the way of their immediate rescue. And neither were the conventional prohibitions of society. The fact that James belonged to Mrs. Zachariah was not to her way of thinking sufficient reason for James remaining at Good Start when he would be better off at their house. Rita might not agree with her, but that did not bother her. Her sense of property had as yet been a merely one-sided development. She yelled blue murder if any beloved object was removed from her, but she had not yet realized that what she desired to lay her hands upon was not necessarily hers to dispose of by divine right. The sense of divine right died hard in her, and the fact that it was coupled more often than not with the crusading spirit did not make her occasional pilfering any less embarrassing for her family.

She had not relinquished James on Friday afternoon because her conscience had been persuaded, but because even in the midst of tears and temper her good sense had realized that the moment of abduction had not yet come. But this wet Monday the opportunity was hers. She seized it with a promptitude and skill remarkable in one so young.

"Please may I be excused?" she asked Miss Bose in the middle of the handicrafts lesson, which was irritating her extremely. It was Miss Amos's half-day off. Miss Bose looked down at Gitashri's crimson face, out of which her father's grey eyes looked up in desperation, and thought peacefully that a period of brief separation between the handicrafts and Gitashri would be good for both of them.

"Yes, Gitashri," she said, "but you must be back in this room in five minutes."

"Ten minutes," said Gitashri who had in mind a

short trip to her country behind the willow fronds, dripping today with diamond droplets.

Miss Bose, who, beneath the new serenity, was still Miss Bose, quelled the giggling of the class with a sharp look and said firmly, "Five minutes."

Gitashri glowered and slid to the floor from a chair rather too high for her. She had every intention of being away fifteen minutes. But out in the hall she knew with a sudden dismay that even if she went behind the willow fronds today, she would not be able to travel to that other country. She knew it intuitively, as a horse knows he cannot take a fence too high for him and balks and turns aside.

In her disillusionment and naughtiness she was in this instant much older than she had been last week. She was the Gitashri she would be in a few years' time, longing for that country but not able to go there anymore. Where should she go? Where James was, of course, towards the forbidden territory of the upstairs landing.

When she got there she did not like it. The only light came from the hall below, and through a close dirty little window curtained with ivy outside and cobwebs inside. It was murky, stuffy, and chilly. The landing was carpeted with a mud-colored oilcloth, and the drafts that came from under the tall brown doors ran over it and coiled themselves about Gitashri's ankles like slimy, moist snakes. At the end of the landing the back stairs fell away into blackness, and up them came a dirty smell compounded of faulty drains, stale food, and damp. Outside a closed bathroom door a pool of water lay on the floor. To Gitashri, standing at a distance, it looked thick and horrible like blood, like a frightening picture of Darnley's murder that she had seen once in a history book; and what was that form lying there with arms flung out and head tipped back, groaning and gasping? And whimpering too. Or was it someone else who was whimpering? Some little boy who was slowly being put to death like the other horrible picture of the princes in the tower?

For the first time in her life Gitashri was in the grip of intolerable fear. She felt sick and dreadfully cold, and a little rivulet of fear was running down her back. She wanted to cry out, but her throat had closed up and she could not. She wanted to run away, but her feet would not move. She was lost and cast away in this evil place and there was no help for her. Her country was gone and home was gone and she was alone.

She began to edge backwards towards the top of the stairs again or else that thing on the floor would get at her. But plucking up the last of her courage she looked again and this time she saw it for just what it was: a pile of dirty clothes lying on the floor waiting to be counted for the laundry. And the pool of blood was only a pool of water. She knew where she was now, not lost but just on the upstairs landing at school. And that wasn't someone groaning but someone fast asleep and snoring behind that half-open door. And it wasn't a little boy whimpering but a dog. It was James! She stood still and listened, courage returning as the crusading zeal burnt in her once again. She followed the noise of the whimpering to a half-closed closet and dimly saw James in a shivering heap on the floor. She snatched him up, scuttled past the snores again and pelted down the stairs as fast as she could.

Now what was she to do? She had been gone a long time and Miss Bose's handicrafts class would be over any minute now. She went to the corner of the hall where the satchels and umbrellas were kept, picked up her satchel and thrust James inside. Just as she had done so, the bell rang and Miss Bose emerged into the hall. Gitashri turned round and said most untypically of herself, "I've taken very long."

"So I observe," said Miss Bose. But looking

down at Gitashri, her whole mind was captured by the attitude of the child. Something was very wrong with her.

"Are you ill, Gitashri?" she asked gently.

"Yes. I want to go home."

"Run along then," said Miss Bose, "I've just seen your mother come with the car." Gitashri picked up her satchel and ran. It was all she could do not to throw herself into Gargi's arms, but without even looking at her mother, she bundled herself and her satchel into the back seat.

"Aren't you coming to sit by me, precious?" asked Gargi, for Gitashri's place was usually by her.

"No, thank you," said Gitashri politely. Gargi was more puzzled than anything but by then Rita and Pia were out too. Rita sat by her mother and Pia, in a dream of her own, did not even notice the heaving of the satchel on her younger sister's lap.

———

At the cottage Gitashri immediately scrambled out of the car and ran upstairs to take off her school things. Pia went to find Kunal and Gargi turned to Rita. "What's the matter with Gitashri?" she demanded, "she wasn't herself."

"I expect she had a dust-up with old Bose," said

Rita. "She asked to be excused from class and went and played games in the willow tree. She does, you know, when she's bored."

"How very naughty of her," murmured Gargi.

"Well, they must go somewhere," said Rita. "Pia just moons around. I'm leaving so I don't care."

"About what?" asked Gargi sharply.

"I told you before, Mummy," said Rita, "that Good Start is a foul, stinking hole." She ran indoors before her mother had time to expostulate, and Gargi put the car away and followed her in that low state of mind familiar to parents whose children are beginning to get out of hand. Bringing up children, she thought, was like pouring beer into a tumbler. All went well up to a certain point, and then it frothed over the top. It was only Rita so far. Pia was not the frothy type but she still had Gitashri down at the bottom of the tumbler.

"Tea is in the kitchen, Gitashri," she called upstairs.

"In a minute," came Gitashri's voice.

The tea was nearly ready before Gitashri reappeared, and then she came so quietly that her footsteps were lost in the sounds of the kitchen.

"Look, Mummy," said Gitashri behind her mother's back. "For you."

Gargi turned round and beheld Gitashri nursing the smallest, fattest, and most unattractive apso she had ever seen. It was old with a grey muzzle and in very poor condition. She had never seen such a horrid little dog and she hated to see such an unhealthy creature held against Gitashri's breast. "Put it down!" she commanded.

Gitashri obeyed and James gave a little whimper of pain, staggered, and then righted himself. He wagged his little bedraggled scrap of a tail. That gallantry of a hurt animal, that instinctive determination to make the best of things, was Gargi's undoing. Revulsion was lost in pity and she sat down on the floor, lifted James to her lap, and examined him for the source of his pain. She did truly love animals. The touch of James's pink tongue upon her hand, as he acknowledged with gratitude her desire to help him, moved her beyond belief.

"Who gave him to you, Gitashri?"

"No one did," said Gitashri. "I just found him. He's for you."

Gargi fondled James's ears and he yelped with pain. So that was the source, she thought. She con-

tinued to fondle him. He was one of the dogs of
Lhasa, noble creatures, who in the days of their
glory had paced in a double line behind His Holiness, the Dalai Lama, the Son of Heaven, holding up
his robes in their mouths. A dog of holy lineage, de-
scendant of the Buddha's lion who, for the love of
his master, had changed himself into a little dog that
he might nestle in his arms. And now come to this!

"Did you find him on the road, Gitashri?" asked
Gargi, "and what were you doing on the road?"

"He was lost," said Gitashri.

"Then we ought to take him to the police station," said Gargi uncertainly. "He is a valuable little
dog."

Gitashri was immune to such a suggestion. "I
brought him for you, Mummy," she said stolidly.

James was set on the floor and lapped at a saucer
of milk hungrily. Gargi and Gitashri sat back on their
heels and watched him.

"What on earth!" asked Kunal. He and Pia had
come hand in hand into the kitchen, and hand in
hand gazed with startled eyes at the object on the
floor. Pia, even more startled than her father,
opened her mouth, and then shut it again. Like Brer
Rabbit, it was her habit to lie low and say nothing.

She had found that amidst the many complications of life, silence was best.

Kunal looked at his wife. With the dog by her she seemed to have shed ten years of her life and there was a glow in her eyes that he had last seen when, as a new bride, she had seen the drawing room. James was soon settled on a cushion and his fate began to be debated. Just then Rita burst into the room. She had nothing in common with Brer Rabbit. Her method amidst the complications of life was direct challenge.

"Good lord!" she ejaculated, "how did James get here?"

"You know the dog?" asked Kunal mildly.

"Yes, of course; he's Mrs. Zachariah's dog for his sins, poor brute. But if you pinched him, Gitashri, there'll be a stink of a row when the old girl finds out."

"He's Mummy's now," replied Gitashri unperturbed.

Kunal drank a little tea to give him strength and then said with as much sternness as he could compass, "Gitashri." His youngest bit into a slice of bread and honey and smiled at him sweetly over the top of it.

"Gitashri, you must tell Mummy where exactly you found that dog."

Gitashri masticated a large mouthful at her leisure and then replied, "Upstairs at school. It was dark and horrid there and I was frightened. There was someone snoring, but the dead person was only a lot of dirty clothes." She then set down her mug of milk, after draining it and prepared to roar. But just as she got her mouth open and her eyes screwed up, and started to take the first deep breath, Kunal interrupted with, "Now stop that, Gitashri. Tell me why you wanted to give James to Mummy."

Gitashri, endeavoring to shut off the roar, got entangled in her deep breath, choked and hiccuped, frightened herself, and began to cry. Between the sobs of her genuine distress her anxious parents caught the broken phrases: "James was hurt in the dark cupboard. She doesn't love James. I hate school. I won't go back ever if Miss Amos is not there. Rita called me a thief but James had to be stolen." She then picked up a currant bun and threw it at Rita.

There was nothing to be done now but to remove her, which Kunal did, shutting her in his study. Tenderhearted parent though he was, he had little compunction about it. There was no grief in these

seizures of Gitashri's, only self-defense and a determination to get her own way.

When he came back it was to find only Rita enjoying her tea. Gargi and Pia seemed to have lost
their appetites. "As soon as we have finished, one of
us must telephone Mrs. Zachariah and set her mind
at rest about her dog," Kunal said to Gargi, "and
then I'll take him back. Gitashri had better not see
him again."

"I wish I could have kept him," said Gargi in a
low voice. "He's such a sick little dog."

"Mrs. Zachariah feeds him on chocolates. How
can you expect such a dog to keep in condition?"
said Rita to no one in particular.

James, asleep on his cushion, whimpered.

"If we took him for walks and fed him right, he'd
become a nice little dog, wouldn't he, Mummy?"
asked Pia.

"Probably," answered Kunal for Gargi, "but
will you telephone now, Gargi, so that I can take
him back?"

Gargi got up reluctantly and went out into the
hall. When she got back she was ashen and trembling. "What's the matter, Gargi?" asked Kunal, all
concern.

"She cut me off."

"Righteous indignation?"

"No. She said, 'Keep the brute, you smug little landlord's wife . . .' Kunal, she sounded as if she was drunk."

"Nonsense," said Kunal.

"She was horrid, Kunal. I thought she was such a sweet old lady."

"Did you?" asked Kunal.

"Didn't you?"

"No," said Kunal, "but without any evidence to support my doubts."

"Why didn't you tell me?" asked Gargi.

"Would you have listened?" She looked at him and saw that he was unsmiling.

"No," she said, and suddenly collapsed in his arms in a storm of tears.

"Whatever is the matter, Gargi?" Kunal demanded. "Is it the kids? If you feel like that about Good Start we'll take them away at the end of the term."

"It's you," she sobbed.

"Me?" asked Kunal.

"You're quite right. I wouldn't have listened to you. I didn't listen to you when you said you didn't want Pia to go back to school today. Why do I always think I know best about everything? It isn't as

married Kunal; not happily but steadily. She had achieved a certain pattern in her life and thoughts, forced it down upon her inner discontent and restlessness, and subconsciously she knew that a change in pattern might mean a change in outlook; and her outlook had not until tonight allowed for the possibility of error in her own judgement. It had been a sustaining outlook that had kept her well afloat on the surface of things, and she did not want to lose it.

There is a certain kind of weather that can arrive in March with the east wind: blue sky and pristine sunshine, birdsong and new leaves on the trees, but repeated day after day—beautiful but going nowhere. Then the wind shifts into the southeast, and a tremor passes over the hard, bright world as it waits for the wind and a short, hard rainfall that will break up the old pattern and make a new one holding within it the promise of a long, tedious summer ahead.

Gargi felt this same tremor in herself. There was to be change. Vikram's return, the mistake she had made over Good Start, even the coming of the little dog had all shaken her. Against her will, her outlook was veering like a weathercock. The wind and the brief rain were coming and she did not know what they would do to her. She looked at her little daughter in the bath, a lovely sight, and her heart suddenly sang for joy. She laughed and forgot her fear.

It was now time to help Vidya to bed, to get the dinner and help Rita and Pia with their homework. Kunal was out tonight and she finished her chores in a leisurely fashion.

In the kitchen she prepared a hot cup of milk for Vidya and went upstairs with it. "Thank you, my dear," said Vidya to Gargi. "That'll do me a power of good. Sit down, Gargi. It's early yet."

It was generally Kunal who took Vidya her milk, and Gargi had a sense of unfamiliarity as she sat down in the little armchair by Vidya's bed. She lived her life in such a rut of routine that the unusualness of what she was doing was yet another thing to make her feel jolted out of herself. Living as she did in a state of perpetual nervous exhaustion, always driving herself beyond her strength lest the tasks of home and the principal's wife accumulate beyond her ability to cope with them, afraid to relax lest she collapse altogether, she had largely lost the power of wonder and with it the power of looking at familiar things with fresh appreciation. She had not really looked at Vidya for a long time. Now she looked at the old lady and thought, "She's got something. I wouldn't know what it is, but some sort of wisdom." Vidya looked fresh and dainty and above all, relaxed. It struck Gargi suddenly that, in having Vidya as part of the household, Gargi herself possessed something rich. Suddenly she said, "You're wise, Vidya," and there was an appeal in her voice as well as the statement of a fact.

"No. I haven't had much education. Not like Kanan who has been everywhere in the world. If you asked me where Rochester was, I wouldn't be able to tell you. Nice for that young fellow to be staying with Kanan. . . . Not young exactly." Vidya's abrupt changes of subject could be disconcerting, and Gargi was disconcerted. Vidya noticed it and waited. Then she asked, and there was pleading in her voice this time, "You'll let him stay won't you, Gargi? Summer's coming on and it will do him a power of good to stay on at Mohurpukur."

"What do you mean, Vidya?"

"I have queer fancies," said Vidya. "Seeing you out in the garden with him I felt you had it in your heart to send him away. You're a proud woman."

"What has my pride to do with anything?" asked Gargi.

Vidya's hands were trembling a little. Never had

she ever criticized Gargi before. "Proud folk separate themselves from others, judging them," she
said at last. "You can't help it, love, but you're too
critical of Kunal, too critical of the children. To crit-
icize others we must hold them at arm's length so to
speak. And then, before you know where you are,
you've pushed them away and you're the poorer."

"This time, Vidya, you're wrong," said Gargi.
"The fool that I am, I told him to stay."

"I don't think that you'll regret it," said Vidya,
"why should you?"

"I was engaged to him once when I was young,
Vidya," said Gargi, and then stopped, aghast at herself. She seemed to be passing beyond her own control.

There was a deepening of the kindly lines in
Vidya's face. "Does Kunal know he was not your
first fancy?" she asked old-fashionedly.

"Yes," said Gargi, smiling, "but what he does
not know was that my first fancy was Vikram Sen.
And he has taken a fancy to Vikram and thinks he can
help him and so I can't tell him."

"Why not?" asked Vidya, a twinkle in her eye.
"Knowing that poor man had been jilted by you
should make Kunal the sorrier for him."

There was a silence. Gargi's lips were folded in a

hard line and Vidya's eyes became extremely penetrating.

"I implied to Vikram that I wouldn't tell Kunal,"
said Gargi. "He likes Kunal."

"Ah," said Vidya, so much in the tone of one
who has at last found out the riddle of the universe
that Gargi looked up, startled. "Now why, my
dear, should you still dislike a man who jilted you so
many years ago that it's a wonder you even recognized him?"

"He hasn't changed," said Gargi. "And I can't
think one kind thought about him."

"What are you letting him stay for, then?" asked
Vidya.

"He seemed such a child suddenly, you know.
But his calculating cruelty once was not that of a
child."

The tone of Gargi's voice shocked Vidya but she
gave no sign. "Children can be cruel, yes," she con-
cluded reluctantly.

"You've lived with children all your life, Vidya,"
said Gargi. "Except for Kunal who does not count,
you don't know men."

"Don't I?" asked Vidya, "and why should Kunal
not count?"

The question shot out with such sharpness that Gargi was taken aback.

"You know what I mean, Vidya," she said weakly.

"I do not," said Vidya. "Is a man less of a man because he's learned to hold his tongue? Though, mind you, I think he's wrong. If Kunal had given as good as he got it might have done you a lot of good."

"I have no idea what you mean, Vidya," said Gargi coldly but with eyes blazing.

"There are some people," said Vidya, "who don't realize what it is they are doing to others until they are paid back in their own coin. But those are not the worst. The worst are those whose unkindness is calculated as you said just now."

Gargi mastered her anger and tried to listen. Vidya went on thoughtfully: "Fear can make you very selfish, you know. What you call calculated cruelty often has its roots in fear. I don't think that the fear you share with the whole world warps you. It's personal fears that do that. Was Vikram afraid even in those days?"

"He had reason to be," answered Gargi slowly. "His first play would have taken away your appetite; but the crowd we moved in thought he was brilliant and I wanted him to be brilliant and successful.''

"Did you push him?'' asked Vidya gently.

"No . . . no. He wrote weird things but Calcutta seemed to love him. He wrote for the open theatre 'Muktangan' and became all the rage. I had my work cut out for me—he was as popular as his plays. I think that people were intrigued that so young a person should have so bizarre an imagination. He'd be full of vitality one day, and great fun, and the next day he'd be drifting about like a lost spirit. And his good looks had the same sort of contrast. He was so wiry and energetic and yet he had the sort of grace the makes people appear fragile when they've got the toughness of a rhino.''

"Well, I'm listening,'' said Vidya. "When was it that you stopped wanting his success and went mad all in a moment for the fire and steel of his body?''

Gargi was shocked, but it was too late to stop now.

"I never did. It was always his success that was the aphrodisiac.''

"And did he realize it?'' asked Vidya.

"He must have. I returned his ring. It was an emerald. And then I sat back to wait for him. He came back to me six months later. I had won, or so I thought. He proposed to me again but confessed he had sold the ring. He had been away on a cruise to Crete. Anyway, this time he came armed with a funny little pearl flower ring and the marriage license. It was a Wednesday evening. We were to have got married on Friday. On Thursday afternoon there was a ring at the door of my flat. I was living in Lansdowne then. I went to the door. It was a messenger boy with a carelessly scrawled note that just said: 'I'm sorry, Gargi. But I can't do it.' "

Vidya was silent. Such a blow breaks a weak woman; twists a strong one. From the angle of her intolerable humiliation Gargi would have looked askance at everything that had happened to her ever since.

"You poor thing," said Vidya.

"Yes," replied Gargi bitterly, "it was just like a scene out of Vikram's own plays."

But that was not what Vidya had meant by "poor thing." To be taking it to heart after all these years. Never to have forgiven, and not told a soul; oh the pity of it!

"What did you do, come morning?"

"My friends rallied around and sent me off to my Kushari relatives. Vikram had disappeared. I came around slowly. And then I sent for Kunal. Has all this made you dislike me very much, Vidya?"

"You know I've always loved you," said Vidya. "You and Rita I've loved most after Kunal."

"Not Pia?" Gargi asked. "Not Gitashri?"

"No. I liked your courage. It has a certain quality. Why don't you tell Kunal the story?"

"Vidya, how can you say that after all I've told you?"

"I don't believe a word of it, dearest."

"Vidya!"

"I mean I don't believe a word of the interpretation you put upon it. There's Kunal returning." Her indomitable little figure relaxed against the pillows. Both their minds had fallen over the edge of the waterfall and passed through the whirlpool below. With the sound of Kunal's step it was as though they had reached calm water again.

Vidya said from against the pillows, "Don't tell Kunal if you don't want to. But neither emeralds nor pearls are your kind of stones. You are a diamond person."

CHAPTER FOURTEEN

"Are you in love, Vikram?" asked Miss Kushari.

Vikram started and looked up from his plate of eggs and toast at Miss Kushari whose face was all but obliterated behind the enormous old silver coffee-pot.

"Return to me, you fugitive jasmine of the forest,
Your absence makes the tears of your
Beloved moon
Overflow,"

he murmured, half blinded by the coffee-pot with the sun upon it.

"No doubt about it," said Kanan Kushari, "I've asked you twice to pass the toast and only the love-sick or the mentally deficient quote Himanshu Dutta of all poets at breakfast."

"I don't know, Miss Kushari," said Vikram honestly. "My trouble is that I have too many doubts."

"I'm glad you recognize the condition as being trouble," said Miss Kushari dryly.

"Yes, I do," said Vikram. "Without doubts, your mind gets fouled. Look at Cervantes. He was a man of faith but he also had his doubts, and nothing fouled Cervantes, not even war and slavery. He wrote the first part of *Don Quixote* in prison."

Miss Kushari, who had known about what he was telling her before he was born, laid down her toast and listened with great courtesy.

"And look at me," Vikram went on. "In the shadow of cell walls I wrote nothing. Before that, deliberate trash."

"Did you write successful trash?" asked Miss Kushari.

Vikram smiled at her bleakly. "Yes. Very smart and clever. Gilded dust."

"You should be able to write here," said Miss Kushari. "It's quiet."

"It is and I am. Quiet."

"Will you write me a good, meaty thriller here?" asked Miss Kushari.

"I'll try," said Vikram, "meanwhile, what

would you like me to do today? I fed and groomed Vimla before breakfast.''

"You might clear away those nettles that are choking the starry jasmine bush. Weeding the front garden is an impossible job, but that particular jasmine bush has always associated itself for me with the poems of Himanshu Dutta, the others and the one you were quoting just now. The whiteness of the jasmine and the moonlight are soulmates. . . .''

"Yes, I'll do just that.''

Miss Kushari continued: ''Today one or more of Kunal's girls will come to visit. And my lawyer, Narayan Singh.''

It was not Vikram's business to ask her why but he was sorry for the shadow on her face. He cleared away the table and washed up. Then he went out into the garden and found a somewhat recovered old Kishun glowering at a pot of petunias. Kantak was there, too, lying on his side, the sun pouring down on his exposed flank. He thumped his tail on the stones when Vikram approached, but did not move. Warmth was what he liked most at his time of life. Vikram bent to pat him before he turned to gloat over his petunias. After he had made contact with his bank manager, plants and seeds had been his first gift to Miss Kushari. He had sent for every kind of flower and already the terraces were a blaze of color in his mind's eye.

"Nothing ever comes to good in them urns," growled Kishun.

"I filled them with fresh earth," said Vikram. "Pass the spade, Kishun. I'll dig, and you can pass me the plants and tell me what a ruddy fool I am."

Kishun growled again. He liked Vikram. The young chap was a hard worker and teachable. Nor had he put himself forward at all. Except in this one matter of petunias in the urns, and in that Kishun had let him have his own way. They continued to dig and to plant.

"Kishun," said Vikram suddenly out of a long silence, "ought a man to forget his own vile actions?"

Kishun's hazy eyes were puzzled as those of a child, and he made no answer. He knew nothing about vile actions. Vikram thought he had never been in the presence of a man who possessed such a depth of innocence. One could almost bathe oneself in it, as one bathed oneself in the soft air of Mohurpukur. And why not? The worth of one man was surely as much at the service of another as the warmth of the sun, if that other had a sufficient realization of his need of it. "And I have, God knows," thought Vikram as he planted the last petunia.

"That's the lot, Kishun," he said. "If you don't want me for anything, I'll tackle the weeds below, especially around that jasmine bush."

"You can't do no harm among them weeds," encouraged Kishun, "nor yet you won't do much good either; not under a twelve-month. But Miss Kushari is particular fond of that white jasmine bush . . . and it's good exercise . . . Sir," he added suddenly and went off round the corner of the house, trundling the barrow. Kishun did occasionally let fall tokens of respect and always when Vikram was feeling most disintegrated by a sense of his nothingness. They seemed to be bestowed to join him together again, for Kishun seemed always moved by that strong creative impulse that only the best men have. In most men, Vikram thought, even decent men, the destructive impulse is strongest in the presence of weakness.

Thus knighted by Kishun, Vikram attacked the nettles and bindweed round the jasmine bush with exhilaration. Kishun had "salaamed" him before, he had opened gates for him, but he had never yet said "Sir." Upon this day of silver sunshine the accolade had fallen.

An hour later, exhausted but triumphant, he sat

down on the wall of the paved court, sleepily relaxed in the sun, and contemplated the result of his labors. He thought it good, for like all amateur gardeners, he did not worry about the roots he could not see. The whole bed below the wall was (above the ground) clear, the lemon bush could breathe and the sun could reach the impatiens that grew about the roots of the jasmine bush. The bush itself astonished him, for, freed from the mass of weeds that had dwarfed its height, it seemed to have grown in power and dignity. It was so old that its main stem and branches were twisted and looped like those of wisteria. Yet the small leaves grew thickly and the shape of it was like that of a standard lamp. It shone against the blue sky with strength and brilliance. Nothing fugitive about it; not the ghostly beloved of a mourning moon, but a virile and entirely masculine presence.

He was half asleep on the warm parapet when he woke to see grave, grey eyes looking at him out of the jasmine bush. Was he awake or wasn't he?

"Chameli?" he asked gently.

"Yes, it's me. But you know me as Pia. Why did you call me by that other name?"

"Because the name is you. Come out from be-

hind the bush will you? Chameli of the poet Himanshu Dutta was a very flowery lady. Do you know the
poem about her?''

''Yes. Aunt Vidya called me after her.''

Vikram repeated the second verse, bending over
to pick a sprig of jasmine.

> *"The bent moonbeams lowered*
> *And mingled themselves with*
> *The pollen of*
> *the Jasmine,*
> *'But,' said the evening star,*
> *'how will you capture her fugitive mind?' ''*

He looked at her and saw that her eyes were wide in
wonder as she looked at him. She was, he realized,
being treated as a woman by a man for the first time
in her life, but she was neither mischievous nor coy,
merely full of wonder as to what this new thing
could be. He saw her delicate beauty, just like the
jasmine's, and was suddenly very happy. He smiled
at Pia and was met with a smile of such delight that it
startled him.

''Are you going to stay with us, I mean with Aunt
Kanan, for a long time?''

''Until I wake up,'' said Vikram.

"I know what you mean," sighed Pia.

"Do you," Vikram answered, rather than asked.

"Yes, I do. It's nice to be asleep. Then things don't bother you, your own problems, arithmetic, Miss Bose. Your parents' problems, very little money, college difficulties. And it costs so much to buy books and pay the professors. Though most of them work for free. Yes. It's nice to be asleep."

Vikram's heart bled for this bruised little jasmine. "But there are nice things in life too, aren't there, Pia?"

"Of course. There's Papa and Mummy. This garden. Mummy's drawing room, both Papa's aunts, and we have a new, old dog."

"What kind?"

"An apso. As a matter of fact he's here visiting Aunt Kanan with my younger sister just now."

CHAPTER FIFTEEN

Only his great age, which made him reluctant to exert himself, and his sense of duty as a host, kept Kantak from seizing the thing as though it were a rat and shaking it until it died. He had never seen such a creature and scorned to give it the name of "dog." He sat back on his haunches, outraged, and looked down his nose to the thing beyond. Not far enough beyond. He could smell it overwhelmingly. He could see it more than enough. With every quivering hair he knew it had come to stay as a member of the family.

He would say for it that it implored permission. Cringing there on the stones before him, not only the whiskers but the whole obese body quivered and the eyes behind the fringe must be terrified. It was the size of a biggish cat and its color was actually a pleasing golden brown. Kantak growled slightly and the thing in a paroxysm of alarm rolled over on its back on the stones, its ridiculous forepaws clutching at its chest and its hind legs stretched out in a manner expressive of the depth of its abject humility. Its chest, like Kantak's own, was white. He had a soft spot for white-chested dogs. Shirt fronts always gave an added air of distinction to a gentleman, though they increased the vulgarity of the mixed breeds. Was this a gentleman? He advanced his nose half an inch and definitely smelled good breeding. There was grey on the muzzle, for, like himself, the creature was no longer a callow youth. It was just possible they might have something in common. He relaxed, and his jaws parted in so tolerant a manner that the creature's parody of a tail trembled slightly on the flagged stones; he relaxed further, and the tail fluttered, still more, and the tail thudded. He lay right down and James rolled over and crawled a little nearer; he closed one eye and James slobbered with relief. Kantak closed the other and James crept as near as he dared. He lay down as well. They communed together.

"Sir," said James, "I had a bad home and now I have a good one with relatives of yours. I live with them who will keep faith. I adore them; especially my mistress. Sir, I have found a refuge for my old age."

Kantak replied, "Sir, you may remain."

"Is it all right?" breathed Gitashri.

"Deep has called to deep," said Miss Kushari. "It's a question of mutual recognition of good breeding."

Aunt Kanan and Gitashri were sitting on the parapet of the terrace when Mr. Narayan Singh, portly and fair, walked up to them.

"You get younger every day, Miss Kushari," he said with deep gallantry, "and you, my dear Gitashri, how you grow!"

"My good sir, children do grow," said Miss Kushari with asperity. "Sit down, Narayan. Gitashri, do a *namaste* to Mr. Singh and then take James around. I want to talk to Mr. Singh."

Gitashri went away with James in her arms and Miss Kushari turned to Mr. Singh. "How is your gout?" she asked, her asperity infused with a sudden kindness. Narayan Singh's compliments had always annoyed her, but he had been her faithful friend for fifty years and he was now her guest. She waited with genuine anxiety for his answer.

"So so," sighed Mr. Singh, his fat hands on his knees. "I am not as young as I was."

"A mere seventy," said Miss Kushari. "I remember you in your perambulator. Will you take anything? A glass of sherry?''

"No, dear lady, not on any account," said Narayan Singh. This routine had gone on for years.

"Then smoke if you like," said Miss Kushari. Narayan Singh puffed in silence for a few moments. He was the very picture of kindly benevolence, but the eyes behind the glasses were very shrewd. Miss Kushari had discovered through many troublesome years that if she disregarded his advice, she was sorry afterwards.

"Miss Kushari," he said, "there's nothing we can do this time."

"Are you quite sure?" she asked quietly.

"Quite sure," said Narayan Singh.

Miss Kushari also lit a cigarette and smoked serenely for a few moments and gazed upon the garden with seemingly untroubled eyes. But Narayan Singh, observing her acutely without appearing to look in her direction, was well aware that this was a bad moment, without being the worst. It was the same for him, and he could not himself put the situation into words. It was she who did that for him.

"The Big House must go on the market," she stated.

"Unless your nephew can enormously increase his contribution to its upkeep," said Narayan Singh.

"You know he can't do that," said Miss Kushari. "He gives more than he can afford already."

"Will you explain the situation to him or shall I?" asked Narayan Singh.

"Neither of us will at present," said Miss Kushari. "For my sake he would be most painfully distressed and plunge into some quixotic action that might ruin himself but do no good to me. You know what he is; one of those halfway cases: neither sufficiently a saint, nor sufficiently a sinner to have much sense. Oh yes, saints have sense, when they are really saints. It is surprising how sanctity clears the mind. Narayan Singh, I am talking for the sake of talking."

"No, Madame," said Narayan Singh. "You have given me an idea. Would you like saints to live in this house?"

"What do you mean?"

"The Shrine at Bodh Gaya. It is not so far from here. I had inquiries from the Japanese Consulate. One of their sects would like to open a monastery in these parts."

Miss Kushari listened in silence. Narayan Singh was a very clever man. Not once in her life had she found her confidence in him misplaced.

"And how is your son in Dubai?" she asked and the conversation turned to more general topics.

———

Driving back to Ispatpur in his shining little Fiat, Mr. Narayan Singh thought chiefly of Miss Kushari. He understood her very well. It would not be the loss of what she possessed that might break her, so much as the loss of the sphere of the usefulness she possessed over the village of Mohurpukur, which had grown to fit her like her own body. The Big House and her own heart alike received their guests, alike gave them their courtesy and warmth. He feared for her leaving the Big House. The Big House had grown with her growth. In a new house growth would have to be something willed and wrought. And would she be able to do it at her age? Those who loved her, and he considered himself among them, would have to make considerable and well-considered demands upon her.

He was thinking of the nature of these demands as he drove past Good Start; here his thoughts were deflected, for Mrs. Zachariah had been a client for many years. It was he who had succeeded her husband as solicitor at Ispatpur. He had heard that she was not well, though not sufficiently indisposed to have sent for the doctor. So far as he knew, she had made no will. Why was that? In his experience those who made no wills either had nothing to leave, feared death too much to face up to its preliminaries, or had so little imagination that, unless some sudden shock brought it home to them, they could not visualize it in connection with themselves. Leaving Good Start behind him, he tried to put Mrs. Zachariah out of his mind, for in spite of her unalloyed sweetness he did not like her, and did not at all want to be summoned to her bedside to help her make her will.

"Hey you damned idiot!" he yelled suddenly and swerved his car into an old fence and an elderly lady picked herself up from the ditch gingerly. An old Ford V8 coming from the wrong direction hit Mr. Narayan Singh's car. A tall figure reared up beside him and an agitated, well-known voice smote his ear.

"It was entirely my fault, Narayan!" said Kunal Kushari, "is the lady hurt do you think?" The tall elderly woman walked towards them and in her turn received both their profound apologies. No, she was not hurt at all. Only the strap of her sandal was broken.

"Then can I drive you anywhere?"

"I live quite close by, Mr. Kushari. At Good Start I teach your daughters."

"Can you possibly be Miss Bose?" asked Kunal eagerly.

"Yes," she said, astonished to see him as warm and confident as he had hitherto been nervous and distracted. A smile flashed over his face. The elusive but much-wanted Miss Bose was delivered into his hands! Beneath his joyousness he was painfully moved by her face. Looking away from her as he opened the car door for her, he saw it as he had seen Vikram's, with that strange visual gift of his that seemed to stamp a face upon the very air and sunlight, so that the light made the truth of it clear to him. The mouth was not actually cruel but it had that thin-lipped bitterness of unhappiness that has found no help anywhere, no outlet but the distillation of itself, acid drop by acid drop, in word and thought and act. The eyes had looked straight into his. He thought that the mind behind the eyes would not flinch from truth, however unpalatable. He wanted to hear the voice again. He believed it had beauty.

"I'll drop you at Good Start, Miss Bose. But would you say it was time also for a cup of coffee?"

"Six and a half minutes past eleven," said Miss Bose, "yes, I'll give you a cup of coffee."

"Here we are," said Kunal turning in at the Good Start gates, "and I am entirely at your service."

The sudden precision of his tone surprised Miss Bose. Her amused liking for the amiable muddler was infused with a sudden respect that was not lost when he stopped the car with such a jerk that her head nearly went through the windshield. He was out of the car in a moment, apologizing and helping her out in a manner that could not have been more courteous had she been a queen. Four shallow steps led up to the front door of Good Start and such is the power of suggestion that Miss Bose walked up them as though she were a queen and led the way to the drawing-room with an air of elegance and grace that smote Kunal's heart with profound compassion. Another man might have thought her air merely laughable, contrasted with her shabby clothes and ravaged face, and the dusty, stuffy room to which she brought him, but to Kunal it was as though he saw a fine and delicate flower struggling for life in some airless slum.

"Please sit down," said Miss Bose, "and I'll ring for Paulina to bring some coffee."

He sat down, struggling with a hideous depression. It had been a delight to find Miss Bose but, as usual, his joy had been short-lived. Never had he felt so utterly inadequate, such an abysmal failure as he felt in this room.

He had been in it before upon some gala occasions with other parents but then the room had been prettied and there was such a concourse of clean children and proud parents that the room itself could not emerge. Now he saw it and felt it: sluggish, unclean, and deceitful.

"This is a horrible room," he said in a quick whisper to Miss Bose.

"It is a vile room," she agreed, also in a whisper and then they both started guiltily as Paulina came into the room. Kunal looked at Paulina pitifully as Miss Bose ordered the coffee. He had seldom seen a more slovenly maidservant, and she obeyed Miss Bose insolently. Yet she did not disgust him as the room did. However much the weakness of one human spirit may be dominated by the strength of another, it retains somewhere its own wavering individuality, but a room takes on the stamp of its owner as helplessly and surely as soft wax. He hated the room but not Paulina.

"Poor woman," he murmured to Miss Bose when she had gone.

"She can be managed," said Miss Bose, "she has the strength of the Santhal tribal in her." This time Miss Bose's voice was grating and had lost its beauty. Kunal started and looked at her. Since their meeting until this moment she had been relaxed and softened, now she was taut with anguished control. He felt her strength, but it was less than the strength that had so long inhabited this vile, deceitful room and it was now very nearly exhausted.

"What a time you must have had," Kunal said, "holding things together here. Trying to give the children some sort of an education, impose some sort of discipline. Well, you've an ally now in Miss Amos."

"I don't suppose she'll stay," said Miss Bose bleakly. "They never do."

"Why do you stay?" Kunal asked.

"Partly because at my age I'm afraid of not getting another job. But chiefly because I'm accustomed to it here. You must think that very odd."

"No," said Kunal, "you are in a state of physical weakness and in such a state it is so much easier to function in the groove you know. It seems to hold you together. I know. I'd be terrified now if I had to cease to be the principal of Mohurpukur College."

"Yet surely that's work you love."

"No, no, dear lady. It was simply thrust on me. And I make such a mess of my job and you do yours so well."

"No," said Miss Bose. "I've become embittered. One can admit to no worse failure than that, can one?"

"I think so," said Kunal. "Embitterment shows a failure of humor, of humility but not necessarily of tenacity. If you still know how to hold on you can redeem what's lost."

"Even love? I detest the children now."

"Children are frequently detestable," agreed Kunal equably.

"I have been cruel to your daughter Pia."

"Yes, I know," said Kunal and then said no more because Paulina came in with the coffee, and he sprang up and took the heavy tray from her, putting it down on a table beside Miss Bose; crooked so that the milk slopped over. By the time Paulina had fetched a cloth and mopped it up, and accepted his embarrassed apologies, she was his friend for life.

"It was not Pia who told me," he went on, when Paulina had gone. "She would never have told me. She has her own kind of strength."

"Yes, she has, and if I had not lost the power of love, I think I should now be finding Pia the most lovable child in the school," said Miss Bose. She spoke in a tone of flat despair and then said, "Mr. Kushari, you must dislike me very much."

"No," said Kunal. "You know, Miss Bose, you're all wrong about yourself. People who have lost the power of love don't grieve over its apparent loss. They don't even know that they have lost it. Hold on and the tide will turn."

"Hold on to what?" asked Miss Bose.

"To grief," said Kunal.

Miss Bose got up and went to the window. She opened it. Because Mrs. Zachariah had always kept it closed, she had forgotten that it could open at all. It was a beautiful day outside.

"Was there anything you wanted to ask me, Miss Bose?"

Miss Bose turned to him gratefully. "It's Mrs. Zachariah. She's not exactly ill, but she's come over all queer. She's in bed and won't get up. She won't exert herself in any way at all."

"In what way did she previously exert herself?" asked Kunal.

Miss Bose wondered if he intended sarcasm, but when she looked at him, he was only wanting to know.

"She sat in this room as headmistress of Good

Start,'' said Miss Bose. "She had a strange sort of strength."

"Yes," said Kunal.

"This term is nearly finished," said Miss Bose. "The Easter holidays are short, and what are we to do next term? Miss Amos and I can hardly take her authority from her and run the school as our own."

"It is a little difficult for me to give advice about next term. My children are not returning to Good Start."

Miss Bose looked at him. "You're quite right," she said. "Good Start is not the best place for them. Nor am I the best teacher for them."

"If you were headmistress of Good Start I would not take them away. In your own school I believe you would make an excellent headmistress."

"You cannot believe that," said Miss Bose. "Not after what I've told you."

"I can believe every possible good of anyone with the power of self-knowledge. But we're getting away from the problem. What are you to do about next term?"

"Mrs. Zachariah won't bestir herself. She won't answer letters. She won't sign checks."

"It's certainly very awkward," said Kunal. "Is Narayan Singh her lawyer? He must be."

"I don't know. She's so secretive about such things."

"I'll talk to him. Good-bye, Miss Bose. Thanks for the coffee."

Miss Bose heard his efforts to get his car started and then the bumping and the creaking as it jerked itself down the drive and out into the road. She leaned back in her chair and laughed and then suddenly cried; tears of quite inexplicable relief and joy. The future was just as obscure, but it had no darkness in it.

———

"Remember it," said Vikram to himself. "Remember this room, the light, the afterglow in the fields and the evening star, the voice of the river below the hill. The books and the white page under your hand. When you go back you can take this with you. Nothing is lost that is stamped upon memory. You may lose it for the time being, you may go mad and curse and rave, but something worthwhile that has once entered your memory is never effaced. Take this and be thankful for there will be plenty of hell for you when you leave this place."

He looked up and saw a bent old man, clean

shaven and in brown robes regarding him. Vikram could have been dreaming.

"Is that the river one hears?" asked the old man.

"Yes," said Vikram, "would you sit down?"

"No, no," said the monk with a touch of shyness, "it's late and I don't want to intrude. I just want to get the feel of this place."

Why, wondered Vikram. Aloud he said, "I wish you would come in though. And sit down."

"Thank you, but my brothers await me. And I am accustomed to standing long hours. One recites the 'Songs of Milarepa'—one stands long hours." The monk bowed deeply and moved away like a shadow.

Vikram stared first at the doorway through which the monk had vanished and then at the empty page before him. On it he wrote of himself. "I've doubts about you, but at least you are now something to have doubts about."

CHAPTER SIXTEEN

*T*t was Monday morning again and Gargi was gardening in the company of a contented mynah. Kunal was at Ispatpur attending a meeting and was to have lunch at the Ispatpur Club. The children were at school. She and Vidya were going to have a lunch that needed no cooking and all the things she ought to have been doing she had decided not to do. These last presummer days could not last and she was not going to miss the chance of a morning's gardening in peaceful loneliness. "I am as contented as the mynah," she thought to herself, "what is happening to me?" A shadow fell across the bed and the mynah flew away. She looked up and said, "Vikram," gently.

He looked at her, smiled, and said, "I'm trespassing."

"Did you want to talk to Kunal?" she asked, "because I'm afraid he's in Ispatpur."

"I wanted to talk to you."

"Then come over here," she said. "Sit on the grass and lean against the gulmohur tree. And don't mind that I shall go on weeding."

Vikram laughed. "Gargi, you haven't changed. You always knew how to talk nonsense while a man got himself to the point. I always admired your social sense."

"What's the point, Vikram?" she asked.

"The truth," said Vikram. "I behaved abominably to you once. I want to tell you why."

"Do you want to tell me for my sake or for yours?"

"I think for both our sakes. For your sake I'd like you to know that I am even more despicable than you thought I was, and be thankful to your merciful stars that you married Kunal. He is . . . your class, if you don't mind the outmoded word. For my sake, if that is possible, I'd like your forgiveness."

"You have it already," she said.

"I'm a coward, Gargi, and of all things I'm terrified most of poverty. I needed money to back a play and I met my late wife, Keya, who would give it to me but for a price. So I sold myself and ditched you. It's as simple as that."

"I did not know you had been married. But why 'late wife'?"

"She killed herself rather than live with me. She never had much of a sense of proportion, you know."

"Neither has Kunal. But that's another kind of madness," said Gargi. "But, Vikram, what a ghastly thing to have to carry with you all your days!"

"Pretty ghastly. But, Gargi, what has come over you? Won't you flagellate me about Keya?"

"I don't have the right to. You see I was in love but not with you, only with what you stood for—success, fame, and so on. I won't deny that your rejection was a blow or that I married Kunal on the rebound. But if I had known your reasons I might have even been happy for your choice. . . ."

"Been happy for my choice?" he asked incredulously.

"Yes. My aunt-in-law, Vidya, to whom I told the story showed me things in the right perspective. Pride does not bleed faster than unrequited love, but it bleeds longer. I know now that I did not love you. So please, Vikram, let us laugh at ourselves and get well."

Vikram smiled. "Gargi, this has been the most astonishing half hour. And I'll try to do what you say.

After all, Mohurpukur is a country where miracles
are possible."

———

Kunal's meeting had been followed by lunch at the
Ispatpur Club, at the invitation of Narayan Singh,
but even the light roast chicken and vanilla ice
cream, chosen by his host as likely to elevate the
spirits but not upset the stomach of a nervous and
sensitive man, had done nothing to make him feel
less wretched. There was a private mental home on
the outskirts of Ispatpur and both Kunal and
Narayan Singh were members of its committee of
management. Once a month they debated its affairs
and talked to its inmates, and once a month Kunal
was plunged into such misery that Narayan Singh did
not know what to do with him.

"Why did you go on the committee?" he asked
now in slight irritation, as Kunal toyed with his ice
cream.

"But for the grace of God there go I," said
Kunal.

"They are not as unhappy as you think they are,"
said Narayan Singh.

"If they are half as unhappy as when I was in Calcutta doing my research and trying to overcome the

longing for alcohol that had overtaken me, they are unhappy enough. But the ice cream is excellent, Narayan.'' And Kunal smiled sweetly in apology. Narayan Singh accepted the unspoken apology and Kunal went on, ''You must see a lot of sadness in your profession, Narayan?''

''If you mean Mrs. Zachariah, and I have been waiting for you to broach the topic, I should feel no sadness at her funeral,'' said Narayan Singh with rosy, smiling honesty. ''But I do not at all look forward to interviewing her this afternoon and persuading her to sign that power of attorney.''

''I've let you in for this, I'm afraid,'' said Kunal.

''You have,'' said Narayan Singh, ''and had better accompany me.''

''No, Narayan, no!'' implored Kunal. ''I'm no businessman, you know that.''

''I do,'' said Narayan Singh, ''and I am not requiring you in that capacity. But you have excellent persuasive powers. If I cannot persuade the old lady to put pen to paper, you may have better success. I told Miss Bose and Miss Amos that they must send for the doctor with or without Mrs. Zachariah's permission. Were she to die without having seen a doctor they would be severely censured. I wonder how they got on.''

The question was answered when the door was opened to them by a tired-looking Elizabeth. "It was hateful when the doctor came," she said, "Mrs. Zachariah shouted at him. It was horrid."

"She should be in a nursing home," said Narayan Singh.

"That's what the doctor said," said Elizabeth. "He thinks she's very ill. But how can we persuade her to go? Do you think you could, Mr. Kushari? Your kindness is so rational, which is really a paradox, I've always felt . . ." and Elizabeth stopped. Both Kunal and she were terribly embarrassed.

"All in good time," said Narayan Singh. "First, I'll have a talk with her on the subject of this document. There's Miss Bose; good afternoon. Is your patient ready to see me?"

"As ready as she'll ever be," said Miss Bose gloomily. "I'll take you up now."

"I'll ask for your assistance if I need it, Kunal," said Narayan Singh. "I may be able to manage alone." And he mounted the stairs with a buoyancy that filled Kunal with profound admiration. Narayan was a very brave man. But in a few minutes, Narayan Singh was back.

"Kunal, I think you had better come upstairs," he said and such was the urgency in his voice that

Kunal went with him at once, with hardly any sensation of dread. He was generally all right once the
trumpet had sounded.

"Yes?" he asked.

"Neither Miss Bose nor I can do anything with
her. She must be entirely crazy. We'll wait outside
on the landing while you have a try. She has merely
to sign her name either to a deed of attorney, or if
she doesn't like that, to a few checks. See what you
can do."

Miss Bose opened the door and Kunal went in and
shut it behind him. "Good afternoon, Mrs. Zachariah," he said and sat on the chair beside the bed.
The hot, stuffy, luxurious room did not affect him as
the drawing room had done, because his whole mind
was focused in dismay upon Mrs. Zachariah herself.
He did not know her, for the mask had gone. The
sweetness, the placidity, had vanished leaving her
speechless with rage, shaking with it, her face purple, her hands plucking at the soiled quilt. But what
he saw in her eyes was fear. A terrible fear. Yet was
she dying? No one had told him so.

He himself was at a great distance from this
woman. Nothing he could do or say would bridge
the gulf because there was nothing here to appeal to.
There was nothing here but anger and fear, things in

themselves entirely sterile. He had not realized before the ghastly evil of negation. He had seldom felt such evil. Nothingness was a bottomless pit and that was what she feared. He began to understand her a little. She was not crazy as Narayan Singh thought. To sign that paper giving the power of attorney to either Miss Bose or Miss Amos was to part with the one possession that she still had in this world. Power.

While she refused to sign, she had the power to paralyze the life of Good Start. Her next of kin was a brother in Australia in whom she was not interested and who had no interest in her house or possessions. To refuse to sign would keep both Elizabeth and Miss Bose entirely dependent on her. Once she had signed it, she would be nothing and be consigned to nothing.

Yet Kunal found himself making the usual appeal. ''Mrs. Zachariah, it would be doing a kindness to the school, to Miss Bose and Miss Amos if you would sign this paper. And to Paulina, too, who needs her wages. If you prefer you can sign a few checks. But you've said I believe that you don't want to be bothered with that. Look, here is your pen. I'll hold the paper for you.''

She took the paper from him and with all the

strength in her body tore it across in half. Then, with an effort ghastly to see, she reared herself up to fling the scraps across the room. She fell back, sagging heavily to one side. Kunal felt as though he were in a nightmare but lifted her gently to the pillow. Her dead open eyes were still full of terror.

———

For the next days Vikram did not leave the Big House garden. This lovely weather would soon break in heat waves, and while the clemency of the skies lasted he must clear the brambles and the weeds from the beds and paths of the garden so that the Kushari children, his Chameli of the forests, Miss Kanan Kushari, and the calf, Vimla, could walk here under the moon. Miss Kushari seemed strangely detached these days. She was as delightful a hostess as ever, she busied herself as usual with her housework and Vimla, her herb garden, but he felt a change in her. She was not in any way losing her grip on things, for he felt a new resolution in her but it was a resolution towards detachment. Vaguely uneasy, he gardened madly and thought of the old monk who had appeared out of the dusk and talked to him at the library door. He kept picturing him in the garden. Once or twice he could have fancied that

he heard his footfall on the flagged path behind him.
He had very soon discovered that one can have very
odd sensations while gardening. A close union with
the earth seemed to involve one in a good deal more
than the earth.

In spite of his unease about Miss Kushari, of his
anxiety as to what Kunal was thinking of him these
days—for Gargi and he had decided to make Kunal
aware of the past—these days were happy for him.
Gargi's strange, sudden softening, the completeness
of her forgiveness, had come upon him like rain
upon parched earth. He felt immensely eased and as
ready to receive whatever the heavens sent as he had
never before been ready. Now he wondered if there
was any conceivable situation in which one could
say—it is the end. Was the word "hopeless" one
that ever had any truth in it?

"I'd like to ask Kunal," he thought. But could
even Kunal forgive his treatment of Gargi? His cow-
ardice? His greed and his ultimate treatment of
Keya? The garden was darkening about him and the
song of the birds seemed to be receding. He went
indoors to find Miss Kushari. She was getting supper
ready. These days she delighted in preparing meals
that were a little different, served on special dishes
and in different rooms of the Big House.

"Kunal rang up with a message for you," she said.

Vikram's heart leapt. "Yes?" he asked.

" '*The Knight of the Wood.* Chapter ten, paragraph one. I'm making a Spanish omelette.' Kunal's mad. But I suppose a message like that makes sense to you."

"Yes, it makes sense," said Vikram and ran upstairs whistling.

He was gay through supper and through washing up. Miss Kushari went to bed early as usual and Vikram almost ran to the library. There was *Don Quixote* on the shelf. He found the passage and read it.

"Sir," answered Don Quixote, "I have so great and hearty a desire to serve you . . . that I might know from you whether the discontents that have urged you to make the choice of this unusual course of life, might not admit of a remedy; for, if they do, assure yourself I will leave no means untried, till I have purchased you that ease which I heartily wish you . . . If then good intentions may plead merit, or a grateful requital, let me entreat you, Sir, by that generous nature that shoots through the gloom with which adversity has clouded your graceful outside; nay, let me conjure you by the darling object of your wishes, to let me know who you are, and what strange misfortunes have urged you to withdraw from the converse of your fellow-creatures, to bury yourself alive in this horrid solitude . . . And I solemnly swear,'' added Don Quixote, ''by the order of the Knighthood, of which I am an unworthy professor, that if you so far gratify my desires, I will assist you to the utmost of my capacity, either by remedying your disaster, if it is not past redress; or at least, I will become your partner in sorrow, and strive to ease it by a society in sadness.''

Vikram put the book down and laughed. The message of friendship and encouragement was unmistakable. They had forgiven him; they had unitedly forgiven him! Tomorrow he would go down to the cottage.

———

The scene that greeted him at the cottage was indeed a strange one. Kunal was atop a tall ladder and trying to tie a long red scarf to the branch of a tree. Rita was holding the ladder and when she saw Vikram she let go of it. ''It's Mr. Sen, hullo Mr. Sen!'' Kunal toppled backwards as Pia hurriedly held on to one of his legs and Gitashri's screams rent the air. But the red scarf, by some miracle, was in place in the branches of the tree.

Kunal got off the ground, rubbing his hands together to shake off a lot of mud and a little blood. "It's Miss Amos," he explained, "coming to lunch. She's Gitashri's class teacher and although a staunch Roman Catholic, she has leanings towards the Left. The red scarf is to welcome her. Join us for lunch, Vikram."

"It was my idea to put it in the tree," said Rita.

"It's my scarf," said Pia.

"My Miss Amos," said Gitashri.

"The disaster of the fall alone is mine," said Kunal humbly.

Elizabeth arrived and Kunal was introducing them and Elizabeth was saying that they had met before. Her eyes were alight with fun as she asked, "And how's Vimla?" But Vikram could not return her smile. Nor could he find the words with which to excuse himself and go away. And then it seemed as though the children and Kunal and Elizabeth closed about him and bore him with them up the drive. The power of their goodwill seemed immensely strong. There was some occult purpose here and he abandoned himself to it in sudden contentment. Gargi met them at the door, elegant and cool, and smiled a blessing on Vikram as if they were friends who met daily and put her arm around Elizabeth with charming elder-sisterliness. It was difficult to feel unease for long in these circumstances. Kunal upset the salad bowl and Gitashri clamored for something or the other. As the scene was set for comedy, Elizabeth looked across the table and smiled tranquilly at Vikram.

"He's beginning to forget my existence and the devils that have been at his heels," thought Gargi. "Well, that's right and very good for me."

"And in the end how easy it is," thought Vikram, "how easy these Kusharis have made everything for me."

CHAPTER SEVENTEEN

*M*rs. Zachariah's brother, Mr. Errol, a Sydney businessman, flew up from Down Under for his sister's funeral. Hearing that Miss Bose wanted to start a school, he signed a lease giving her Good Start at a nominal rent for the next ten years. He had no interests in India and wished Miss Bose the best. He presented her with all the contents of the house, shook her warmly by the hand, and leaving all further details to Narayan Singh, departed again for Australia.

"He looked such a dried-up stick you wouldn't have thought he'd be so generous, would you?" said Elizabeth.

"People are generous," said Miss Bose, "look at yourself, Elizabeth. Mr. Sen wants to marry you and yet you are insistent on living here, helping me get started. Isn't that generosity?" After a while she added, "And you can't really like me at all."

"Yes, I do," said Elizabeth, "I didn't. But now I do."

"Why?" asked Miss Bose.

"It's all part of it, I suppose."

"Part of what?"

"The interweaving," said Elizabeth.

"I've never been able to see much pattern in life myself," said Miss Bose.

"Nor have I," said Elizabeth, "but I do know that the interweaving of one life with another is life's painkiller. Look at Vikram. These Kusharis have recently pushed him through the eye of the needle and he has come out safely the other side. As for me, I always intended marriage for myself. I just didn't know I'd fall so madly in love first."

———

Up at the Big House Miss Kushari was sitting in her drawing room with Narayan Singh. She had on a Kashmiri silk sari, diamonds in her ears and on her fingers. There were fresh flowers in all the vases. Yet, though outwardly bedecked and serene, she was inwardly troubled. "I can't get used to the idea," she said to Narayan Singh. "It's some comfort that they will only rent this house. It's not gone forever. And they'll pray in it."

"Nothing is settled yet," said Narayan Singh. "You're just going to have a talk with the monk and let him have a look at the house. His order may make you an offer that you may not think suitable. Nothing is settled. It is just as unsettled as the weather."

"Which is very settled at the moment," replied Miss Kushari tartly.

A shining Datsun had driven up to the front door, a young monk at the wheel and an old monk beside him. Narayan Singh went out to welcome them; Miss Kushari stayed where she was. She looked round her drawing-room and knew a moment of sudden and abject misery. Until this moment she had not fully realized what she was doing. Her mind had known that she must leave the Big House, her will had resolved to do it, but while she made her decision, and while she set up the necessary machinery to carry it out, her home had been holding her close as it had always done. In every sorrow of her life the Big House had held her and until now she had not realized that in this sorrow, the Big House would hold her no longer. Now full realization smote her. She got to her feet as the door opened and came forward, but for the first time in her life she was a tongue-tied hostess.

Only one monk had come in, and she heard him say that Narayan Singh was showing Lama Ai the garden. She supposed they had shaken hands. She found they were sitting down. A harsh voice was croaking in her ears, "You have lived here all your life, Madame." Miss Kushari looked at him. He was bent like some old tree and his habit was the color of the bark of an old tree. His face—she had not known a face could be at once so ugly, so attractive, so humorous, and so relentlessly austere. She was aware of a great kindness in him. His hands were swollen with rheumatism.

"The climate should suit your rheumatism," she said. "It's mild and the house is high enough above the river to avoid the damp."

"What I have to discover," he said, with a touch of sharpness, "is not the suitability of the climate to rheumatism, but to the life of prayer, Madame. I understand," continued the old man, "that in the last resort the decision does not rest with you?"

"It rests with my nephew," acknowledged Miss Kushari, "but it was for my sake only that we have struggled along here so long. Had it not been for me he would have sold the Big House long ago. To save him distress I am conducting these preliminaries without his knowledge."

"When you have conducted them is there any likelihood that he may refuse his consent?"

"Kunal is accustomed to having practical matters arranged for him behind his back by his womenfolk," said Miss Kushari. "He is that type of man and his wife and I are that type of women."

"No sons?" asked the monk.

"He has no sons. The line of Kusharis dies with him."

"I had imagined the young man a son of the house," said the monk, "he seemed so entirely happy here."

"What young man?" asked Miss Kushari.

"I confess I came here the other evening after Mr. Singh had spoken to me. And there was a young man in the library. He seemed to blend here."

"Oh, that was Vikram, my guest. He will live in the village in future. He is marrying a girl from Ispatpur who teaches and loves little children. Vikram himself is a writer. They will build a house down there, see, where the river Ruprekha makes a reefknot by winding round itself. Did you know that a reef-knot gets tighter the harder you pull at it? Right over left and left over right."

"Do you mean it will be a happy marriage?"

"Not necessarily. It will be a marriage with staying power. Frank Amos's daughter has life force.''

''And you, Madame?''

''I will build a small house atop that knoll there. My cowman lives there now. I will build him a sturdy hut. My calf, Vimla, and my old dog, Kantak, will stay with me. Mine will be an air-filled house, strong and small. And that Vimla always had a tendency to walk down the steps here. On the knoll there will be no danger.''

''Then the money my order will give to your family will make amends for your having to leave,'' said the monk.

''In many ways,'' said Miss Kushari. ''Kunal's cottage can be renovated and the college will have funds. The girls can go to good boarding schools when the time comes and I from my house will hear your chanting. What may I call you?''

''I am His Holiness the Reverend Lama Ugen.''

He looked at her for a long time and then said, ''Call me Brother.''

''As you say. By the way, do you chant the 'Songs of Milarepa'?''

''Yes. All one hundred thousand of them.''

Miss Kushari began to feel content.

*I*t had been a year of many changes. Old Paulina no longer felt old. She was dressed in a light-blue starched sari with a dark-blue apron over it and carried in Miss Bose's tea to her on a spotless tray. Miss Bose and Miss Amos, or rather Mrs. Sen, worked her harder than she had ever worked before, but under Paulina were two other maids whom she in turn worked hard. And she felt content. Good Start was clean and airy; the windows open. The children were much the same but the whole place now had a sense of direction—as if things were heading somewhere.

Miss Kushari's house atop the knoll was ready and geraniums and petunias cascaded from it as if it were itself a stone urn. Next door to her, Kishun lived in splendor. His hut was all sunlight; sometimes he shut the door on one's face but you never could tell.

On the eve of their wedding, Vikram and Elizabeth had been to visit Vidya for the first time. "I need no introductions," the old lady had said. "I know Elizabeth's father and Mr. Sen, I remember what the weather was like the day you set foot in Mohurpukur. It was a grey day and I had been thinking of prisoners, even praying for them. For when there's a grey wall between one and the other who is to say which is the prisoner and which is free?"

"I don't know what you mean," said Vikram tentatively.

"The grey clouds are like men's unbelief," said Vidya, "and men live frozen and afraid, when a touch or a word from another would set them free."

"Many who would like to believe like you can't, Vidya," said Vikram.

"Nonsense," said Vidya calmly. "Remember those cranes that day? How they clamored! They wanted something and they got it."

Vikram looked at the old woman keenly. She had power of a different sort than Miss Kushari's. He began to understand what immense concentration of power there can be in a life that has withdrawn if discipline can keep pace with withdrawal. Without discipline, withdrawal was disintegration.

———

Kunal and Pia trudged up the hill to the Big House. Kunal held a large rolled-up bundle under his arm. He had come to loan his treasures to old Lama Ugen. The Big House looked the same except that everything was in the prime of condition. Flowers bloomed in the borders—especially calendulas— lemon, yellow, and orange. They were said to be the flowers beloved of the Lord Buddha.

Lama Ugen himself opened the front door over which Kunal stumbled.

"I've brought you something," he said, "the tangkas of Milarepa. They would look better here than in my cottage." He tried to undo the bundle and the scrolls fell at their feet, unrolled and opened in all their jeweled colors—red, gold, green—like a chestful of gems.

And old Lama Ugen stood like a child, wondering upward at what fell from heaven to gild his monastery. Years later, Pia would smile and explain the miraculous scene. Nothing was forgotten. Time and seasons reenacted their rites and Mohurpukur remained for those within it a country that distilled happiness and restored souls. At dawn and dusk could be heard the chanting of the monks:

"In Red Rock Jewel Valley
Young sparrows learn to fly
Bees are humming among the flowers,
Intoxicated by their fragrance
All friends of Milarepa
Drink the nectar of kindness and compassion
Then return to your abodes."

ABOUT THE AUTHOR

Until her death in 1993, INDRANI AIKATH-GYALTSEN was a freelance journalist and hotel owner in Darjeeling. She is the author of *Daughters of the House*.